BEFORE THE TRACKS WERE LAID

LEIA KAY

TO:
My mother, Cathy, for always allowing me to
keep my head in the clouds.

My darling Hooman for being my biggest
cheerleader.

My sister Misty for showing me scary can
be fun.

My children for keeping me young at heart.

I love you all.

HE INHERITS IT ALL

A PEACHTREE PLANTATION NOVELLA

CHAPTER 1

The Beginning

The man who owned the land before William Cheney, was named Huxley. He buried both his sons in the months before harvest. The boys had just come into their strength, finally ready to work the fields. No wounds. No fever. Just gone, as if the red clay beneath their feet had quietly claimed them back.

After that, Huxley wandered barefoot through the orchard for days, his eyes wide, searching the trees like they held a language only the lost could hear. He spoke to no one, but the wind shifted when he passed, and the crows fell silent. They found him hanging from a beam in the smokehouse the next Sunday, mouth still open, as if the truth he carried had turned to ash before he could speak it.

Huxley hadn't always been alone. There were once enslaved men and women on the land. They were bought or borrowed; no one quite knew. But they vanished one by one in the dead of night. Some said they ran. Others whispered they were taken, claimed by the same force that turned the boys to shadows. By the time the frost came, only Huxley remained, speaking to the unseen and waiting for an answer that never came.

That was all the local men needed to know.

But William needed more.

"Two hundred acres for less than the price of good timber," he told his wife, Eleanora, as their wagon creaked along the overgrown path. "The man went mad, not the land."

William had gone to Savannah to collect supplies and finalize the deed. He was only meant to be gone for two nights, but the days stretched long in his absence. The house creaked constantly, as if remembering something. The orchard, thick with shadows, pulled at her gaze. Once, she thought she heard a voice calling her name from behind the smokehouse, but when she went to look, there was nothing there.

He returned on the fourth morning, bringing more than flour and salt. In the back of a second wagon, six enslaved souls sat in silence—four men and two women —bound not by rope, but by the brutal knowing that there was nowhere else to go.

One of them, Sibella, watched the trees with grave-eyed stillness, her profile sharp beneath a faded blue headwrap. She was tall and lean, wraith-thin, like the wind passed through her instead of around her. She didn't blink when they passed the orchard. She didn't speak at all.

"They'll help raise the house," William said. "And everything in it."

· · ·

It was early morning when the wagons rolled in, the sun low and hazy, filtering through the moss like gauze. The air still held the chill of night, though the insects had already begun their slow, humming song. Eleanora stood on the porch with her arms wrapped around herself, watching as the second wagon came into view.

The Huxley homestead, rotting and half-swallowed by vines, had been deemed unfit to live in. Too many boards were warped. Too many doors wouldn't stay shut. William called it unsafe and ordered the new hands to sleep in the old smokehouse and barn until cabins could be raised. He and Eleanora would sleep in the wagon for now, the mattress laid across barrels and crates of preserved goods.

The house was torn down within the week. William watched with satisfaction as the chimney toppled, proud to erase what he called bad history. But when they dug up the foundation, they found small bones tucked inside a rusted tin box, and a child's shoe wrapped in burlap.

The foreman laughed it off as poor

folks' superstition. "Some folks bury dolls and shoes to keep the devil out," he said, tossing the shoe aside like it was nothing.

Sibella didn't laugh. She stared at the box like it had been waiting for her. She bent down, careful not to touch it, examining it from every angle, stood, and backed away.

That night, she tied a scrap of thread around a limb of the old pecan tree and whispered. Her words carried the cadence of the elders, slow and heavy with meaning.

"De land ain't quiet, jus' waitin'."

Eleanora said nothing, but each night, as she lay beside the summer kitchen in the makeshift bed, her hands folded over her stomach, protective and still, as if shielding the child within. She couldn't bring herself to sleep in the new house. The air was too still, the floor too quiet. And in the corner of the room, the cradle sat empty, waiting. Sometimes she swore she heard something breathing beside it, soft and slow, not quite human.

William dismissed it. "You're a woman. It's the baby."

But when the baby came, when William Jr. was born beneath an April storm and the windows shuttered themselves closed, Eleanora understood the house had been listening all along.

The omens had been plentiful, and she was scared for them all. She pressed a hand to her newborn's chest and whispered to no one, "You didn't just inherit his name. You inherited it all."

The land, the silence, the sins buried beneath both.

The weight of what they had taken.

The price no one spoke of.

Outside, Sibella watched lightning lick the edge of the trees, her eyes unblinking. She felt it too. Whatever had settled over the house was not finished. Not yet.

"Blood callin' blood now," she whispered. "An' de roots already know."

CHAPTER 2

Sibella

The land spoke. Not in words, but in the noticing. In the way birds did not sing at dawn. In the way the air carried no scent after rain. In the way roots surfaced, like they were trying to escape.

Sibella felt it the moment the wagon turned off the main road.

She did not look at the man who had bought her. Did not look at the pale wife beside him. She kept her eyes on the trees, gnarled things with bark like cracked bone, and listened.

It was waiting.

"Wuh's bruk cyan be fix, but wuh's cursed mus' stay buried," she murmured to herself on the ride. *What is broken can be fixed. What is cursed must stay buried.*

They were made to carry bricks, to clear vines with bare hands, to haul stone and timber for a house no one wanted to live in. The master said it would be grand. That it would stand for generations.

Sibella knew it would. But not for the reasons he thought.

William worked beside them, sweat soaking through his collar, boots caked in red clay. He spoke little, watching, noting. The hands watched too, but not him. They watched Sibella.

She never gave orders, but they moved when she moved. Took the long way around when she did. Avoided certain trees. Refused to hammer nails into a particular beam until Sibella walked the perimeter and nodded once.

"Feel like de ground listenin'," one of the men whispered while digging the foundation trench. "Like it remember," another muttered. "Like it angry."

Sibella said nothing, but her presence was steady, grounding. She hummed sometimes, low and tuneless, when the work felt too still. And the others found that they worked better when she did.

At dusk, when the shadows stretched too long, they stopped early. No one waited to be told.

That night, while smoke from the cookfire drifted across the field and the baby cried again from inside the wagon, Sibella sat alone beneath the pecan tree. Her fingers brushed the thread she had buried days earlier, and she whispered again.

"Keep what's buried. Keep it deep."

Whatever lived in the land was stirring, and the house they were building would not keep it out.

CHAPTER 3

Delivery

When the moon was behind the Earth and the sun had not yet risen, the sky was black with nothing in it. A scream tore through the plantation. Not the cry of a rooster, but something deeper. Raw. Human. The kind of scream that made men leap from bunks and women drop to their knees in prayer.

Eleanora screamed as if giving birth were tearing her in two. The air turned thick and sour. Even the animals backed away, shifting from hoof to hoof with uneasy energy.

The midwife, Miss Letty, had delivered more babies than she had fingers to count. She stood at the edge of the room for a long time before stepping inside. She was not the kind to scare easily.

But when she came out from the smokehouse where they stayed as the house as built, her face was ashen. Her hands shook as she wiped them on her apron. "Something ain't right," she whispered to William.

William was frantic. "Are they okay?"

"Yes, sir. He's here, but he's too quiet. Eyes too open. Like he know more than he should."

William waved her off and brushed past her, eager to see his firstborn and the wife who had given him life. "Old and superstitious," he muttered. "She's lost her edge."

But he could not sleep that night. None of them did.

Outside, the rain fell without wind. The doors stayed shut. And William Jr. blinked, slow and wide-eyed, as if he had seen something on his way through that he was not meant to remember.

William held him proudly, swaddled in his arms, but something inside him twisted. He had expected crying. Not silence.

Eleanora bled for hours. A fever came, and with it, whispers from her mouth of a name that was not his. Her milk never came. No matter the teas, the cloths, the prayers, her body would not give.

So, Sibella fed him goat's milk, warmed by firelight. She watched the child's eyes the entire time.

By the time the bleeding stopped and the room grew still, Eleanora was able to rest. Her eyes fluttered shut, lips parted as if to pray, but no sound came.

The air did not lift. It shifted.

Not empty. Occupied.

A soft creak echoed from upstairs. No one was there.

Sibella turned her head sharply toward the sound. Then looked down.

The baby was staring at the ceiling.

Not startled. Not confused. Waiting.

She held her breath. He blinked, slow and deliberate, as if he already knew what had made the noise and what it meant.

· · ·

In the days that followed, strange things began to stir. Inside, the baby cried at the walls. And the mother? She wandered the garden path like a ghost not yet dead.

Sibella saw it then. Eleanora's soul already flickering like a flame too close to the wind. Pale lips. Wrung hands. Eyes that searched for something she did not want to find.

"She ain't gone yet," Sibella whispered to the wind. "But she hauntin' just the same."

Later that night, while the rain tapped gently on the shutters and the fire faded low, Eleanora pressed a hand to her newborn's chest and whispered to no one, "You didn't just inherit his name. You inherited it all."

CHAPTER 4

Sibella and Eleanora

It was the child. Not the way he screamed, sharp and thin like he was being born again every time he woke, but the way he stared.

Sibella had seen eyes like that once before, when she was still a girl and her uncle pulled a drowned man from the Edisto River. The man had no soul left in him, just that wet, bloated silence in his face.

The baby looked like that some nights.

She waited until the house was asleep. Eleanora sat alone, rocking without rhythm, her shawl loose, her face hollowed by shadow. The lantern burned low beside her.

"You should let de child sleep near light," Sibella said, voice low and steady.

Eleanora jumped, hand to her chest. "You startled me."

"Didn't mean to," was all Sibella said.

The unnatural silence settled. The crickets didn't sing. The wind didn't rustle. Even the trees, usually creaking in their roots, held still, as if everything stood still, holding its breath.

Sibella stepped closer, careful.

"You feel it, don't you?" she asked. "That thing always beside the boy."

Eleanora's lips parted, but no sound came out. Her eyes flicked to the windows upstairs, then back to Sibella.

"You speak in riddles."

"Not riddles," Sibella said, crouching to press her fingers to the dirt. "Truth don't always come in plain words."

"He's just... colicky," Eleanora said, her voice shaking. "The doctor said some babies cry like that. Boys are harder."

"It ain't his cry," Sibella whispered. "It's what cryin' through him."

Eleanora gasped, stood up sharply, folding her arms tightly. "I won't hear this kind of talk."

Sibella looked up at her, still crouched at the base of the steps, her palm dirty with red clay.

"You already hearin' it," she said. "In the walls. In the floorboards. In your blood, and you know it."

The silence stretched between them like a rope pulled too tight.

Eleanora's voice softened, her posture relaxed. "If I let myself believe it… what then?" She hesitated, then added, "How do you know these things, Sibella?"

Sibella held her gaze. "Some of us born knowin'. Some of us learn when we too young to want it. And some of us just listen close enough to hear what most pretend ain't there."

Eleanora studied her for a long moment. Then she asked, "After all you've been through, why are you helping us?"

Sibella looked away, toward the dark line of trees. "Ain't helpin' you," she said quietly. "Helpin' him. He didn't ask to come here. He didn't choose none of this. That child need someone watchin' when the rest of y'all look away."

Sibella rose slowly. "So you keep him in the light. You don't let him near the place where the shoe was found. And if he ever stops cryin' for too long, you wake him up."

"Why?"

"'Cause quiet don't mean peace," Sibella said. "Not on this land." She hesitated, then added softly, "It ain't your fault he like this. Wasn't nothin' you did. It's where he was born. Somethin' came through with him. Somethin' caught a ride."

She turned without being dismissed, her footsteps soft in the dirt, her shadow swallowed before she reached the edge of the trees.

Eleanora didn't follow. She sat back down and watched the lantern flicker in the windless air.

Upstairs, the baby had gone still again.

And she realized she hadn't heard him cry in nearly ten minutes.

CHAPTER 5

The Baby

Time passed, though it was hard to say how much. The days melted into each other, indistinguishable under the heavy breath of the land. The new house rose slowly, beam by beam, as if even the wood hesitated to take root in that soil.

William was less present. At first, he had worked alongside the others, sleeves rolled to his elbows, face ruddy with sun and labor. He handed out orders with a kind of practiced charm, always reminding the workers it was a "shared effort." But then the deliveries from Savannah needed attention. Then came the issue with the tools, the lumber, the dry goods, and the books he kept in the barn. There was always a reason to be gone, and fewer reasons to return.

The baby was not sleeping. He was lying still, and that was not the same.

Eleanora stared at the cradle until her eyes blurred, waiting for the rise and fall of breath. Sometimes it came. Sometimes it didn't. Sometimes she found herself holding her own breath, as if the two were linked by some unseen thread.

Once, when the baby had gone too long without stirring, she wandered out into the night barefoot and dazed. The sky was blank, starless. She walked to the edge of the orchard and dropped to her knees. She dug with her hands, feverishly, until her nails split, and the soil filled the creases of her skin. She did not know what she was searching for, only that something in her blood demanded it.

Later, she would not remember coming back inside. Only the ache in her fingers, the dirt beneath them, and the way the baby stared when she returned.

She hadn't eaten in a day. Or was it two?

There was no clock in the nursery. William had promised to bring one from Savannah, but he'd forgotten. Or refused. Or lied.

The hours ran together now, measured only by the flickering of the oil lamp and the cries that no longer came.

She pressed a hand to the baby's chest. Nothing.

Then, a breath was shallow and slow, like someone hiding from something.

"He's not mine," she whispered.

Behind her, the floor creaked. The old smokehouse had been hastily cleaned and patched for shelter while the house went up. The boards were uneven, warped from old rain, and cried out with every shift of weight.

She turned. No one.

She turned back. The baby's eyes were open. Staring straight up, as if watching something move along the ceiling.

That night, Sibella came in without knocking. She carried a tin basin of warm water and a bundle of clean cloths, but she didn't offer them. She set them down and waited.

Eleanora didn't turn to face her.

"You ever heard of the changelings?" Eleanora said, her voice thin, like breath through lace.

Sibella paused. "No, ma'am."

"The Irish believe they come at night. They take your baby and leave another in his place. A hollow thing. A mimic."

Sibella said nothing.

Eleanora turned now, slow and wide-eyed. "My grandmother told me about them. Said if the child stopped crying, you should worry. A real child cries. A false one just... watches."

She began to laugh softly at first, then sharply. "And what do we do when our children don't cry? When they go quiet?"

Sibella stepped forward. "You keep him in the light, like I said. You keep your feet out the orchard, and you don't feed the silence with your fear."

Eleanora's laugh died in her throat. "Don't you see? I've already fed it."

She held out her hands, filthy and scratched, the nails torn. "I dug. I dug with my hands. I dreamed of roots curling like fingers around his ankles. Of soil pressing against his chest."

Sibella flinched.

Eleanora sat down on the floor. "He doesn't blink when the lightning comes. Doesn't flinch at thunder. I wrapped him in my grandmother's christening gown, and he screamed like I'd set fire to him."

Sibella knelt, placing her palm gently against Eleanora's cheek. "You ain't mad, miss. Not yet. But the land want you to be."

Tears welled up, but Eleanora didn't blink. "I want to love him. God help me. But I don't know what I'm loving anymore."

Sibella stood, walked to the window, and tied another thread of her headwrap onto the latch."No one ask if the first family had a baby," she said softly. "Only said the boys died. Only said the man hung himself. No one asked why."

Eleanora stared at her, hollow-eyed. "You think something's inside him."

Sibella looked down at the cradle. "I think something wants to be."

She turned, walked to the door, then paused. "Don't put iron near him. Not silver neither. If it's still him, it'll harm him. Iron cuts through things that don't belong, and silver shows what's hidden. If it's not him anymore… it won't care."

She left without another word.

Eleanora sat next to the cradle and stared into her child's face. A small voice in the back of her mind wondered if she was losing herself, if the silence, the sleeplessness, and the things she dared not name were peeling away her sanity piece by piece. She had heard of women slipping after childbirth, of minds unraveling in the quiet. But what if this wasn't unraveling? What if it was waking up?

He looked back, calm, silent, unmoving.

"Tell me what you are," she whispered. "Before I forget what I am."

The oil lamp flickered.

And for just a second, just one, she swears his eyes flashed the color of the orchard soil.

CHAPTER 6

The Root Cellar

It was late afternoon in early May when Sibella waited until William was gone, riding into town for nails, he said, though he never returned with just that. The sky was hazy with sun and dust, and the smell of turned earth hung thick in the air. It should have been planting season. The other workers whispered about it—how the ground stayed still, how no one had been told to sow. They muttered that something was wrong, that the land was waiting for something other than seed. The fields near the orchard remained untouched, the plow left leaning against the fence like a forgotten question.

She watched his wagon vanish down the path and then crossed the yard with her shoulders squared and her jaw tight.

The summer kitchen leaned a little to the left, like it was tired of holding up its own weight. Behind it, overgrown brush covered the entrance to the old root cellar. Sibella moved it aside, stone by stone, like lifting a wound's scab.

Eleanor followed.

Barefoot, her nightgown clinging with sweat and stained from days of wear, she moved like a ghost tethered by a thread. Her hair stuck to her temples. She clutched something in her hand, a silver knife, polished to a gleam. Something sharp enough to pierce a man and sacred enough to ward off what had no name.

Sibella turned at the cellar steps. "You bringin' that to keep you safe?" she asked gently.

Eleanor nodded.

"Then throw it away."

Eleanor didn't move.

"Silver don't help here. Makes it worse."

Eleanor hesitated… then flung the knife into the weeds.

They descended.

The air was thick, ripe with rot and something older—something like memory. The temperature dropped with each step. At the bottom, Sibella lit a lantern. It flickered weakly, as if the darkness refused to budge. A chill moved through the chamber like a wave, slow and steady, rolling through bone and stone alike.

In the corner, beneath a shelf of preserved jars and empty crates, lay a small hollow in the dirt. From it rose the smell of turned earth and something bitter.

Sibella reached in and pulled out a cloth bundle.

Inside: coins worn smooth, feathers, grave dirt, three human teeth. And a name etched into bark—William Jr.

Eleanor recoiled.

"Who did this?"

"I did," Sibella said. "I was trying to bind it to protect him, but I didn't bury the first one. This was done long before me."

Eleanor backed away, whispering, "You said the land chooses."

"It feeds first," Sibella said. "Then it chooses."

Eleanor dropped to her knees. "Why him? Why not me?"

Sibella's face was grim. "You already hollowed out. You hear the land. You see."/

Eleanor's voice cracked. "So he's safe?"

Sibella hesitated. "Maybe."

"Then it took me instead," she said, almost to herself. "It took me."

Sibella wrapped the bundle again. "No. You gave yourself over. There's still time to take it back."

Eleanor stared at her, eyes wide and vacant. "I don't know who I am anymore."

"Then we find you," Sibella said. "Before the land swallows what's left."

Above them, something thudded softly across the floor of the summer kitchen.

Not footsteps. Just… movement.

But it was enough.

CHAPTER 7

The Preacher

He came that following Sunday, before services. The sun had just started warming the sky and burning off the thick morning humid air. This visit was not by chance, William had sent for him. Quietly. Two weeks prior, with a letter scratched on the back of an inventory sheet and sent by a boy on a borrowed mule. After the first night, he found Eleanor outside, without shoes, in her nightgown, scratching at the earth.

There are disturbances on the land. Come if you believe in what can't be named.

Now he stood at the edge of the yard, hat in hand, his eyes narrowed against the morning sun, taking in the house, the fields, and the orchard.

"You got my message?" William asked, stepping off the porch.

The preacher nodded, his voice low. "I did. Thought long and hard before coming."

"I didn't write for a sermon," William said. "I wrote for the truth. You speak on devils and curses; I expect you to do it plainly."

The preacher's jaw worked. He stepped closer, voice tightening. "You know whose land this was before you came."

"Huxley," William said. "No kin. Left it behind after his sons died."

The preacher's gaze darkened. "He didn't *leave*. He hung himself. Behind the smokehouse. Took them a week to cut him down; no one wanted to go near the place."

William's face remained blank, unreadable, hopeful that his wife didn't hear the response

The preacher didn't blink. "He came

from good stock. Had a wife and two boys, Irish Twins, barely out of short pants. Moved here for fresh land, good yield. Brought a nursemaid and two hands with him."

He looked toward the orchard.

"First year was fine. Second year… the boys changed. Stopped speaking. Started drawing things in soot on the walls. The mother claimed they'd been 'touched by dreams.' Said they kept waking with dirt in their mouths."

Sibella and Eleanore, behind the porch rail, turned their faces slightly, Eleanore to listen better and Sibella to read what the preacher was saying without his words.

The preacher hesitated, cleared his throat, and continued.

"She tried to burn their beds," the preacher said, voice gravel-thick, bent his head closer in a voice just above a whisper, "Said they weren't her children anymore. That they'd been *replaced*." He straightened up and looked around, making sure no one besides William heard him. "Said the orchard had taken their souls and left her with looking-glass ghosts."

He paused. Then he shook his head in misery and raised his voice back to normal

"Huxley beat her for the talk. Locked her in the pantry to keep her quiet. So they say," he shuffled his feet, looked back up.

"He never asked for me. I would've told him that she was just touched in the head, is all." He tapped to his temple

Eleanora's breath hitched.

"They say she stopped screaming after the third day," the preacher went on, his voice low and distant, like the story cost him something to tell. "Stopped moving too. When the neighbors finally forced the door open, she was sitting on the floor, head tilted back, mouth stretched wide like she'd died *still trying to scream.*"

He looked into William's eyes slowly.

"But the walls were covered in drawings. Scratched in with a bent spoon. Symbols none of them recognized. Circles inside circles. Eyes with no pupils. A tree with its roots *reaching up* instead of down."

A pause. The preacher scratched the stubble on his chin.

"There wasn't a mark on her. Just her eyes... gone white," said it like a ghost story around the campfire.

Eleanora gripped the doorway like it might carry her weight.

"What happened to the boys?" she asked from her place near the house. William was startled to see her there.

The preacher looked at her, gentle now, walked toward her, and stopped between William and her. "One went missing. Just vanished. The other... was found under the pecan tree. They said he was sleeping. But he'd been out there all night. Cold didn't touch him. Not one bite on his skin."

William crossed his arms. "And the father?" Feeling as if the father was to blame.

"Walked barefoot through the orchard, mumbling to himself for days. Neighbors stopped coming. The hands fled. No one wanted the land. Said it was spoiled."

The preacher looked William squarely in the eyes. "Until you came."

William scoffed. "So I'm to believe I inherited ghosts? I bought a cursed orchard and built my house on bones?"

The preacher's voice was calm. "You bought a mouth, Mr. Cheney. One that eats names and spits out legacies."

Sibella dropped the bucket. The water splashed her feet. She did not move.

Eleanora stepped forward, her voice fragile. "If he knew the land was cursed, why didn't he leave?"

The preacher shook his head. "Because when the land chooses you, it don't *let* you leave. Not whole."

He looked toward the awning, where the baby sat in his cradle, too still, too quiet.

"Mark my words," he said. "That child will carry more than his name."

William stepped forward, fists clenched. "You think I'd write for your help just to be accused in my own house?"

"I think you feel it," the preacher said. "In your bones. I think you wake in the night and wonder if your son's breath is yours or *borrowed*. I think you called me out here hoping I'd say you were mad."

William said nothing.

The preacher turned to go. "You're not mad. But you *are* too late."

When the congregation found the preacher's body that night, having missed service, he was beneath his overturned cart, his fingernails were broken, and his mouth full of soil. The coroner said he'd died trying to dig. There was no grave nearby.

The neighbors sent word of the incident to William, sending a worker's boy, rather than coming over themselves. William didn't speak about what happened to Eleanor; she didn't need to know anything more.

But that night, holding the child like something fragile and foreign, William whispered, "They all want to take you. But you're mine. You hear me?"

His voice was low, hoarse, not a question, not a comfort, but a warning.

The baby didn't look at him.

He looked past him.

Out the window.

Toward the orchard.

A breeze stirred, though the glass panes didn't rattle. The air inside the smokehouse chilled, as if someone had left the door open to something that didn't belong.

William's arms tightened. He looked down, but the baby's gaze remained fixed and utterly still, unnervingly aware.

William swallowed hard.

He didn't speak again.

CHAPTER 8

The Blood Moon

By midsummer, the house stood nearly finished, roof pitched, shutters hung, and floors laid tight with hand-planed boards. But inside its walls, something had begun to unravel.

Eleanora wandered the halls barefoot now, speaking less with each passing day, her mind unwinding like a ribbon snagged on bramble. The enslaved kept their distance, watching her with wary eyes, whispering when they thought no one could hear. Dishes clattered when she entered a room. Doors closed gently, but always just before she reached them. Only Sibella dared to stay near, calm in the storm of Eleanora's fraying thoughts, her voice the only one that could coax her back from the edge.

Outside, the air had grown too still. The birds that once filled the orchard with chatter had vanished. Even the wind, once a familiar rustle through the trees, had not stirred in weeks. It was as if the land itself were stuck, between breaths.

William no longer lingered with his son. Not for long. The boy's eyes unsettled him, too aware, too knowing. Sometimes he'd catch the child staring at nothing at all, or worse, at something William couldn't see. And though he never spoke it aloud, he'd stopped calling him *"my boy"* in his mind. It felt... untrue.

The work continued around them, plaster drying, nails driven home, but none of it quieted the tension coiling tighter by the day. Something was coming. Sibella felt it. So did the others. Even the horses had begun to spook at shadows.

It began with the wind.

As the sun set, the sky lit up like fire in the heavens. After weeks of stillness, it returned all at once, hard, hot, smelling of iron and ash. It blew through the orchard like something searching. It rattled the shutters. It hissed through the chimney, low and coiling, like a snake dragging its belly across stone.

The baby's cry had stopped an hour before.

Eleanora had felt it first in her chest, a sudden sting, like a breath held too long. Something in the house had shifted, and though no door had moved, she felt it: the air thickened, the temperature dropped. The boards beneath her bare feet were colder than they should have been. And in the silence, not even the floorboards creaked.

She turned toward the boy's room. The door stood open just a crack, pale dusk light slanting in across the hallway wall. The new room smelled of milk and fresh plaster, but there was something else now too: charred wood and something faintly sweet, like decay pretending to be perfume.

She crossed the threshold slowly. She glanced at his wooden toys on the floor. Her fingertips brushed the door frame. And before she saw, she *knew*.

The silence wasn't peace.

It wasn't sleep.

It was absence.

It was wrong.

She paused at the foot of the cradle, her hand to her chest, and remembered it was just a week earlier that he had smiled for the first time. Not a flicker of gas or sleep, but a true smile. She'd sung to him, some old hymn without words, and his lips had curled like he understood. His eyes had caught hers, bright and sharp, too knowing for a child so small. That smile haunted her now.

Her breath coming in gasps, she stood at the cradle a moment longer, long enough to hear it. The sound rose from beyond the orchard, low and tuneless at first, then rising into something like a lullaby. But not one any mother had ever sung. The notes were off-warped, as if remembering a melody from a forgotten life.

It all came rushing at her: the red thread, the whispered prayers, the buried shoes. Everything she and Sibella had done to hold it back, to keep it at bay... none of it had worked. "Oh God."

And his bed was empty.

"William!" she screamed, her voice already breaking. "He's gone!"

He was halfway down the stairs when he heard her scream.

The sound stopped him cold. Her voice was not panicked but broken. Not a mother searching for a misplaced child, but a woman who already knew the truth.

His breath caught. For a moment, he simply stood there, one hand gripping the banister, the other clenched white around the lantern's handle. The shadows on the walls seemed to breathe.

No cry. No rustle. No reason.

And still, he knew this was not some midnight wandering. Not a door left ajar. This was something else.

He rushed the last few steps, bootlaces flapping, nearly dropping the lantern in his haste. Eleanora met him at the nursery door, her eyes wild, her face pale and wet with sweat and tears. She didn't speak. She just pointed with a trembling hand.

The cradle stood there, still and open, blanket folded too neatly to be chance.

Gone.

He didn't ask where the child could be. He didn't call out his name. He didn't move.

Because deep down, William already understood. The house had been trying to tell him.

The land had been warning him.

And now, something had answered.

They set off frantically searching the house first, every room, every corner, even the pantry.

Empty.

From the shadows by the kitchen door, two of the house servants stood watching. Ruth, whose hands never stopped wringing her apron, and young Josiah, who looked at Eleanora with wide, unblinking eyes. Neither moved to help. Neither dared.

"They told her to leave it buried," Ruth whispered to no one. "Said those shoes wrapped in cloth weren't meant to be touched. Not after what happened at the Huxley place."

Josiah only crossed himself and backed farther into the dark. Afraid to be seen

Then the door banged open on its own, and the wind slammed into them like a warning.

Ruth took one step backward, then another, until the pantry swallowed her completely. She didn't close the door behind her, just let it drift half-shut, her breath hitching in the silence.

Neither of them would enter that hallway again that night. Not even to fetch water. Not even if fire took the roof.

They knew better.

Because when the wind came like that, hot and full of iron, slamming doors and moaning through the rafters, it meant that something had walked in that didn't belong.

Something had been let loose. Or let in.

From the pantry, Ruth whispered a prayer older than her name. From the shadows, Josiah watched the lantern light flicker and didn't dare to look toward the orchard.

Because the orchard was calling.

CHAPTER 9

Gone

Lantern in hand, William led them into the dark, shoes half-laced, sweat clinging to his skin. His shoulders trembled. For the first time, he looked small on his own land.

"He's out there," he said, voice hoarse. "My boy."

Sibella was already waiting at the edge of the trees. She'd tied red thread around her wrists and carried no light.

"You don't bring flame to a place already burnin'," she said quietly.

William looked at her like a man

seeing something he'd spent years trying not to.

"What is this?" he whispered. "What's been walking in my walls? Breathing in my child?"

Sibella didn't smile. "Now you ask."

He nodded, slow. "You warned me. You warned *her*."

She said nothing.

He swallowed hard, voice breaking. "I thought it was her mind going soft. But it wasn't."

"No," Sibella said. "It was her soul goin' sharp."

The moon rose—deep red and enormous, too close, too low, too *present*. It cast no warmth. Only shadow.

And from somewhere deep within the orchard came the sound of a child… giggling.

Eleanora stepped forward, barefoot in the grass. "That's not him." She turned to William. "But it's wearing his voice."

He blinked at her, lost. "What do we do?"

She closed her eyes. "We give it what it came for."

"No," he said, grabbing her wrist. "We go back to the house. We wait it out."

She pulled free. "It won't wait. It never has."

Back in the kitchen, the air shifted.

Ruth pressed her back to the pantry wall, eyes closed, lips moving without sound. The hair on her arms stood on end, though the heat hadn't broken. It clung to her like wet cloth, thick and unmoving until, all at once, it did.

The wind turned.

It wasn't natural wind, not the kind that cooled or carried storms. This moved like breath, like thought, pressing through the cracks in the floorboards and sighing through the keyholes. It smelled of iron and turned the sweat on her neck cold. Somewhere deep in the walls, the timbers groaned.

Outside, Josiah had crept just far enough to see the edge of the orchard, and what he saw froze him still.

The trees were swaying, but not in the wind. They recoiled, bending backward as if something moved *through* them. The leaves didn't rustle; they *shivered.*

He watched Eleanora step into the first row, barefoot and trembling, and though he couldn't hear her words, he saw the way she threw her arms wide and screamed into the dark.

And then the wind struck the house like a hand.

It slammed the shutters, howled through the eaves, and dropped the temperature so fast the glass in the kitchen windows fogged.

Josiah staggered inside the pantry, eyes wide, slamming the door behind him. He turned to Ruth, who had sunk to her knees in the pantry, clutching her apron tight in both fists.

"That ain't no wind," he whispered.

Ruth shook her head. "No. That's the orchard choosing."

Eleanor continued into the first row of trees, moonlight streaking across her face, the branches bending *away* from her as if startled.

And then she screamed, with all the

weight of the mothers before her, *"Take me! Take me!"*

The wind stopped.

Just like that. Gone, as if the reins were pulled taut.

The orchard, moments ago alive and writhing, fell into a dreadful stillness. Not a leaf moved. Not a branch dared creak. The very air seemed to hold its breath.

The moonlight struck her full in the face, and the trees were tall, ancient things bent back as if startled by her voice.

Even the cicadas fell silent.

A hush so complete fell over the land that Ruth, crouched in the pantry, thought for a heartbeat that time had stopped.

And in that awful stillness, the humming ceased.

The wind dropped. The orchard stopped moving. The air flattened into a terrible, expectant quiet.

William ran to her. Pulled her back. His arms were shaking.

They collapsed in the grass just beyond the trees, his breath ragged. Her eyes were wild.

Holding her with one hand while the other smoothed her hair. "We go inside," he said. "We stay together. We stay in the light."

Sibella met them on the porch, opened the door without speaking. William stepped inside with Eleanora in his arms, her body limp, her head resting against his chest. She wasn't crying. She wasn't speaking. Her eyes stared past him, wide and vacant, as if whatever she had screamed in the orchard had left her hollowed out.

William set her gently on the hallway bench, her body slack in his arms. She didn't speak. Didn't cry. Just stared ahead, as if the world had faded to smoke.

He turned away to lock the door, to bar the windows, to light every lamp he could find, anything to keep the dark at bay.

No one saw her rise.

Not Ruth, who backed down the hall without a word.

Not Josiah, who turned his face to the wall.

Not even Sibella, whose eyes never left the orchard.

At some point in that terrible hush, Eleanora slipped from the bench and made her way to the cradle. Her steps left no sound. Her shadow didn't stir.

She lay down beside the cradle, her body curled like a question, her lips moving in whispers no one heard.

And by the time they looked again, the baby was there.

And Eleanora was already too far gone.

Later, they would find a smear of blood along the floorboards where she'd walked.

Her feet were torn and raw, streaked with dirt and thin cuts, too many to count.

As if she'd come back across something that never meant to let her go.

Sibella lit a single candle and placed it near the cradle. The baby slept peacefully, breathing steadily, swaddled tightly.

They didn't speak the rest of the night.

William sat hunched in the parlor,

boots still damp, staring into the cold hearth as if it might offer an answer. The lantern beside him guttered low, casting long, shivering shadows up the wall. He didn't notice when it finally went out.

Sibella remained in the kitchen, near the back door, red thread still tied at her wrists. She kept her eyes on the orchard through the window, unmoving, as though listening for something no one else could hear.

No one checked on Eleanora.

No one dared.

She lay curled beside the cradle, her head resting on the floorboards worn smooth by the recent hand sanding, her fingers grazing the hem of the christening blanket above her. And her lips moved silently in prayer, plea, or memory, no one could say. She never closed her eyes.

And in the morning, William went in to check on her and realized now that she was gone.

They found her hours later, half-submerged in the stream that ran behind the orchard.

Her skin was as pale as milk. Her hair

fanned around her like moss. Her dress had frozen to the stones beneath her, though the air was warm, and the fields lay bare, untouched by seed.

There was no wound. No water in her lungs.

Only her expression was now soft and peaceful, as if she had simply stepped into sleep. Her torment finally ended.

Back in the house, William Jr. was in his cradle.

Wrapped tight in his christening blanket, Breathing soft. Eyes open and alert.

A tiny red thread lay curled in his hand.

And just beneath the cradle, on the freshly laid floorboards, sat a bent silver spoon, blackened at the tip.

CHAPTER 10

The Funeral Procession

The morning air was heavy with the scent of cotton and decay.

William rose before the sun, already dressed in black. The starch in his shirt had wilted overnight, and the sleeves hung loose around arms that felt more like bone than flesh. He had not slept. Nor would he, not until she was in the ground.

They carried her on a door.

No proper coffin had been prepared. There hadn't been time. The child woke screaming each time they brought her near. So, William and two of the older men lifted her gently onto a wide plank door, wrapped her in her linen shawl, and walked her down the winding path toward the old cemetery clearing.

It was not a marked graveyard, not anymore. Just a patch of high ground nestled among the pecan trees, half-swallowed by ivy and time. But the Huxleys had buried their dead there once, long before madness took the house and rot claimed the orchard.

Sibella walked ahead of them, scattering sage and crushed cedar underfoot. Her hands trembled as she worked, but her steps never faltered.

Behind her, the procession moved in silence. All the hands had come, dressed in whatever dark cloth they could find. Some had shoes. Most did not. None spoke.

The trees overhead hung low with Spanish moss, trailing like funeral veils.

At the center of the clearing, the earth had already been turned. William had dug the grave himself the day before, sweat blurring his eyes, fists blistered raw. He hadn't let anyone else touch the shovel. It had to be him.

When they reached the edge of the grave, he knelt beside it, breath hitching.

He had buried men before. Strangers. Even a cousin once, during fever season.

But not her.

Not the woman who had followed him to this land, who had lain beside him through storms, who had wept into his shirt the night their child came screaming into the world.

He lowered her into the earth himself.

Sibella stood beside him, humming low and mournful. It was not a song William recognized, but the sound made the hairs on his arms rise.

Then one of the elders, an old man named Ben, who had once dug graves for a living stepped forward and bowed his head.

"Lord, take this woman home," he said, his voice rough as stone. "Let her rest from her sorrow, and let her name not be forgotten, even here."

A few heads bowed. One woman wept softly.

William's eyes stayed open. Dry.

He reached for the first clod of soil and let it fall.

Then another. And another.

Each sound of dirt hitting cloth was a thunderclap in the hush of the grove.

Behind him, the child stirred in the arms of one of the older women.

And then, as the last shovelful fell, as the grave was sealed, and the wind slipped through the moss above like a whisper.

The baby laughed.

High, bright, clear.

Not a chuckle. Not a gurgle.

A *laugh*.

William froze.

The woman holding the boy nearly dropped him.

A few of the younger hands stepped back, eyes wide.

Sibella's humming stopped.

Back in the house, where the light no longer touched the nursery window, Ruth stood frozen beside the cradle.

She'd come to fetch the baby's blanket.

What she found instead was the spoon.

Still bent.

Still blackened at the tip.

Lying where it hadn't been that morning.

She stared at it. Her voice barely more than breath.

"It came back," she whispered. "Same as him."

It had been buried with the shoes.

Wrapped tightly in white cloth, sealed in the box found beneath the foundation, unearthed when the foreman ordered the crew to dig deeper for the cellar supports.

Sibella had told them to leave it, said the ground had claimed it for a reason.

But he hadn't listened.

Said it was *"just old things."*

Laughed when she crossed herself.

A week later, the foreman fell from the ladder while finishing the gable. Broke his neck clean.

They buried him in a pine box. Said it was an accident.

But Ruth knew better.

So did Sibella.

And now the spoon was back.

Sibella appeared in the doorway.

She didn't ask what Ruth meant. She didn't need to.

She stepped forward, wrapped the spoon in a strip of muslin, and pressed it deep into the pocket of her apron.

"Don't speak of it," she said. "Not to him."

Ruth nodded once, eyes shining. "I won't."

And the baby, now resting quiet in his crib, stared up at the ceiling.

Still.

Watching.

As if he'd heard every word.

And the grove fell quiet again.

CHAPTER 11

William's Speech

The sun was beginning to set, dragging long golden shadows across the fields.

The orchard leaves had gone dull in the heat, flickering gold in the low light, rustling like secrets.

From a distance, the plantation looked peaceful. Ordinary.

As if it hadn't just taken something from them.

Everyone was still in black.

The house staff and field hands

gathered beneath the awning by the summer kitchen, where the lanterns hadn't yet been lit. A hush clung to the yard, heavy as smoke.

William stood on the steps of the main house, his mourning coat dusted with clay. He looked like a man carved from ash, hollow, brittle, and barely upright.

The baby had been laid in the cradle, now moved into the parlor where the lamps burned high.

No one wanted him out of sight.

Ruth had played with him until his eyes grew heavy, then placed him down for a nap, and kept watch.

The house was quiet now. Too quiet.

As if the land, for the moment, had taken what it came for… and was content.

Sibella stood just to William's side, arms crossed tightly, her shawl drawn close around her shoulders.

She said nothing.

Her gaze never left him, not the crowd, not the child. Only him.

As if she was waiting to see what kind

of man he would choose to be in this moment.

He cleared his throat once.

Then again.

The silence stretched.

"I know… it's been hard," he said finally, his voice thin and strange in the open air. "This land has tested us. We've lost much. More than I could have imagined when we first came here."

No one replied. The crowd was still. Listening. Waiting.

William looked down at his hands. Opened and closed them like he wasn't sure they were still his.

"I don't pretend to understand what's happened," he said. "Only that it… came for us. And it took her."

A flicker passed across the faces in the crowd, grief, recognition, and something older. Something like knowing.

He glanced toward the orchard, then forced himself to look away.

"But it's over now."

He said it too quickly.

Like a man trying to convince himself before anyone else.

"It's over," he repeated, slower this time. "Whatever darkness lived in that grove, whatever sickness followed us here… it's done."

He looked out over the gathered faces.

"You're safe now. We all are. We'll keep on. We'll work the land, raise our children, restore what's broken. That's what she would've wanted."

From the back, Ben shifted his weight. A quiet noise escaped his throat, half scoff, half sigh, but he said nothing.

Sibella didn't move. Her eyes never blinked.

William stepped down from the porch, closer to them now.

"Thank you," he said. "For seeing us through. For seeing *me* through."

Still, no one responded.

Because no one believed it was over.

Not really.

They nodded, out of respect. A few bowed their heads. But their eyes remained watchful, turned toward the orchard, toward the moss-draped trees that had not stopped whispering.

They knew better.

They knew the land never truly let go.
It only… paused.
"Just for now," one of the women murmured under her breath.
And the others nodded.
Just for now

CHAPTER 12

Sibella and William's Pact

That night, the house was still.

Not peaceful, more like *satisfied.*

As if the land, for now, had taken its due.

The baby slept in the parlor beneath the oil lamp, its wick trimmed low but unextinguished. William refused to move him back upstairs. Something about the nursery, about the shadows on the wall and the way the floorboards breathed, was too close to memory.

William sat on the porch, coat

unbuttoned, sleeves rolled. A bottle of rye rested on the step beside him. His fingers trembled as he poured, though he didn't spill a drop.

Sibella stood in the doorway.

She didn't ask permission. Just sat down beside him, her shawl pulled tight across her shoulders. She didn't look at him, but she didn't need to. He was already speaking.

"She knew," he said. "Long before I did."

Sibella said nothing.

"She tried to tell me. Tried to fight it. And I called her weak."

Still, she said nothing.

He drank.

"You were right too," he said. "About the land. About it listening."

A pause.

"I think it wanted her. But it chose him."

Sibella's eyes finally turned to him. "It doesn't choose without reason."

William nodded slowly. "He laughs at graves. Doesn't cry. Doesn't blink at thunder."

He looked toward the trees, now dark and swaying faintly in the wind.

"I don't know how to raise something I don't understand."

Sibella's voice was quiet. "You won't do it alone."

William blinked at her.

"Then you'll help me?"

"I'll watch him," she said. "I'll keep what needs keeping. But don't mistake that for trust. Or forgiveness."

He nodded again, slower this time.

"We tell folks it was fever," he said. "Or a sleepwalking spell. She went to the stream and never came back."

Sibella's jaw tightened. "Folks believe what makes them feel safe. Let them."

He looked over at her, more hollow than grateful.

"Will he ever be normal?"

Sibella looked out across the yard, where the moon threw long shadows across the pecan trees.

"No," she said. "But he can be guided."

Then her voice shifted to quiet but firm.

"You know it took the firstborn from the Huxleys. The little one under the pecan tree."

William swallowed.

"And now it tried for yours."

Sibella's eyes met his. "It always wants the first."

He looked down at his hands. "Why?"

"To mark the bloodline," she said. "To plant somethin' deep."

She stood, her shadow long behind her.

"And in passing down what cannot be carried alone."

She turned to go. But just before she disappeared into the doorway, she added, "One day, someone will come who can hold what he cannot. A child who will carry more than she's asked to. And the land will know her when she steps on it."

William tilted his head. "Someone else?"

Sibella gave the faintest nod. "Not yet. But the ground already stirs. Like it's waiting."

She closed the door behind her, the wood groaning like a closing grave.

William sat alone.
From the parlor, the baby stirred.
Then a tiny laugh rose in the stillness.
It was not cruel.
Not loud.
Just… knowing.

The years moved forward, as they always do...

He grew wealthy.

The cotton came up thick, the hands worked hard, and buyers from Savannah lined up for his yields. The house expanded. New rooms were built. The orchard was fenced off, though no one spoke of why.

But the world beyond the fields was changing.

The war hadn't come yet, but it was close. Whispers rode in with the traders. Words like secession, abolition, and fire.

William Sr. passed first, his face

turned to the window, eyes fixed on the grove.

"It took your mother," he said, his voice thin as breath. "Make sure it doesn't take the name."

Sibella lived on for many years after.

An old woman by then, she had outlived the master and most of the hands she once worked beside.

She died in her sleep, peaceful, or perhaps simply tired.

She left behind no children, only charms tucked in corners, red thread knotted behind doorways, and a whispered warning to William Jr.: "Watch the trees when they bend without wind. And never let the house go quiet."

William Jr. buried them both in the family graveyard, beneath the pecan trees, beside the woman whose blood birthed him and the woman who truly raised him. He had no memory of Eleanora, not her voice, not her touch, but he remembered Sibella's hands, always working. He remembered the way she hummed when storms rolled in. He remembered her warnings.

He heard the warnings but thought them foolish.

Old stories. Frightened whispers.

Things meant to scare children, not grown men.

He married a woman named Alice.

She gave him a healthy son, born with pale eyes and a sharp cry that startled the dogs outside. They named him William, like the men before. But they called him Billy.

And the land remembered.

It remembered the boy who laughed at the grave.

It remembered the woman who offered herself in the wind.

And it remembered the bloodline it had touched, though not yet claimed.

What the land carried, it never put down for long.

WHAT LUCY CARRIED

CHAPTER 1

10 years later…

Before Lucy came to the Cheney House, there was the Carroll place. Her mother, Eliza, had been born into bondage but carried herself with a grace that often made people step back before daring to shout. She taught Lucy not to bow her head unless she meant it, not to speak unless she had thought her words through twice, and to always, always listen to the land.

They lived in a cramped room behind the smokehouse, with Eliza rising before sunrise to cook and clean, and Lucy following behind with quiet steps and bright eyes. Eliza sang while she worked, with hymns laced with warnings and lullabies carved from grief.

"We cross when we must," she'd whisper to Lucy on nights when the woods moaned and the men drank too long, "and we cross with our heads high, even when the water is deep."

Lucy knew what that meant. Crossing wasn't always about rivers. It was about moments. Decisions. Crying out, staying quiet, leaving. Staying. Surviving.

And on the night the wind turned cold and the fire burned low, Eliza bent close and pressed a token her mother had stitched by hand, a cloth that carried warning and warmth into Lucy's hand: a torn piece of Sunday cloth, stitched with roses and the scent of wild mint. "You listen to the land, baby," she said, voice low like a prayer. "If it ever goes quiet in the wrong way…don't wait. Don't blink. And don't run. Just remember who you are and what you came from."

The day her mother died, Lucy was shelling peas by the fire pit. There was a crash inside the main house, followed by a curdling scream. By the time someone thought to fetch her, Eliza was already still. A slipped step, they said. A fractured skull on the stone cellar stairs. But Lucy never believed that. Her mother never slipped, but her mother did see everything. She wondered if her mother had seen too much.

No one packed her anything. No shoes, no satchel, not even a goodbye. So Lucy reached for the one thing that her mother had always kept close: a torn piece of her favorite Sunday dress. It still smelled faintly of wild mint and hearth smoke. She clutched it tight as the wagon creaked down the red dirt road, the only thing she carried from the life they took from her.

That was the day Lucy stopped looking for safety in adults. But she never stopped listening to the land.

The summer sun was already high when the wagon creaked up the long dirt path toward the Cheney House. Dust plumed behind it like smoke, choking the air with heat and grit. The trees along the lane stood still, but not in the way of a calm morning, more like they were listening. Some leaned just slightly in the wrong direction, as if bent by something that had passed through long before the wagon ever came.

Alice Cheney stood on the front porch in her cream morning dress, pressing a hand to her stomach as if to still the hollow ache that had settled there for years. William Jr.—Will as Alice had called him since early in their marriage—was still away on business in Augusta, leaving her to manage the arrival.

Two children huddled in the back of the wagon, silent and far too still for their age. One, a boy, was soon handed over to the overseer. The other, a girl with wide eyes and tight braids, clutched a small cloth bundle to her chest.

"What's her name?" Alice asked.

"Lucy," the driver said, barely glancing back. "Just turned eight. Her mother died on the Carroll place."

Alice stepped down from the porch,

ignoring the heat baking the steps. She bent, lifting Lucy's chin gently with two fingers. The girl flinched.

"She'll stay inside," Alice said without consulting anyone. "With me."

Gently, she took Lucy by the hand and walked up the stairs that radiated with the Georgia heat. Alice held in her shock; the girl didn't even flinch at her bare skin touching the hot stairs. Alice wanted to pick her up so she wouldn't suffer, but she didn't want to scare the young darling. So instead, when they entered the house, Alice handed her a folded linen handkerchief embroidered with soft forget-me-nots and bluebells in the corner.

"This was mine when I was a girl," she said. "It always made me happy to see the pretty flowers, and I hope it will make you just a little bit happier." Lucy looked up with a strength no eight-year-old should ever have to possess, her chin set in a defiant way.

She took the handkerchief; inside, she awed at how pretty the stitching was. She looked at the intricate ways the flowers were embroidered and ran her thumb over them. "Would you like to learn how to do that someday?" Alice offered.

Lucy wanted to so badly but knew that this woman was not to be trusted, so in return, she simply offered a curt "yes, ma'am." She didn't realize how high Alice's shoulders were until she let out a breath, and they came down.

It must have been the right answer because she smiled at Lucy, not a big toothy one, but a kind one that met her eyes. "Come on, let me show you to your own room." This caught Lucy by surprise, but she knew not to show it.

Billy was ten when Lucy came to stay. He watched her the way cats watch birds, not with hunger but with calculation. He never blinked when she looked back. His eyes, too pale, held a coldness Lucy recognized from her bad dreams.

Alice noticed it too: Billy lurking behind doorways and around corners, his gaze lingering too long. At first, she chalked it up to curiosity. Children always noticed new arrivals. But something else coiled beneath his stare, something sharper than interest. It unsettled her in ways she couldn't quite name.

Lucy was quiet and obedient, eager to please. But in the quiet moments, she would braid scraps of cloth into tiny knots and whisper as she did, just like her mother had. "If you are quiet, listen to the land," she would hear in memory. "It tells the truth when people won't."

Alice began to keep her close, having her pour tea, fetch linens, and sit beside her embroidery frame. When Alice read aloud in the afternoons, Lucy curled nearby, her small hands folded in her lap, the handkerchief often tucked under her fingers.

The bond between them grew quickly. Alice brushed Lucy's hair at night and tied a scarf around her head. She also taught her to sort the lavender and rose petals for sachets. She whispered soft prayers from her girlhood. She found herself smiling again.

Their days took on a rhythm of shared silences and soft instruction. Alice taught Lucy how to iron fine lace without burning it, how to press flowers into books, and how to blend herbs into remedies that soothed both body and mind. Lucy picked things up quickly, more quickly than any child Alice had ever known. She handled lavender like a whisper, stitched her name with trembling care, and began reading words from Alice's books with a quiet hunger.

In the garden, they worked side by side, Alice in her wide straw hat and Lucy in one of Alice's old aprons cinched tight around her waist. Lucy talked more there, where the air moved freely and the sky opened wide. She spoke of her mother and how she used to sing to the moon, how she always left bread by the door for the spirits, and how she had once seen a deer cry before it died.

Alice listened, her heart aching with the long-standing guilt she faced every day. She realized then it wasn't just protection she wanted to give this child. It was memories. She wanted Lucy to grow into her own story, not one shaped by loss, servitude, and silence, but by knowing her life held meaning. She couldn't help all of them on her land, but she could try one by one, and Lucy was the first.

At night, when the house was quiet and the fire burned low, Lucy would curl up at Alice's side. Alice would run her fingers over the girl's back and think of that long-lost bonnet in her drawer. But she didn't dream of that baby anymore. Instead, she dreamed of Lucy growing tall, learning everything Alice could impart, and one day sitting in her own parlor with a daughter who carried both memory and hope.

However, before Lucy ever arrived, Alice had known a different kind of ache: the quiet hollow of a mother without a daughter. Years before Billy was born, there had been another child, lost before taking her first breath. A daughter. Alice remembered how small the bonnet had been, the one she had stitched in lavender thread. The bonnet lay untouched in the drawer beneath her winter shawls.

Will had been tender then, for a time. But his patience thinned with the years, especially after Billy arrived. When Alice suggested trying again, just once more, in hopes of having a daughter, Will shook his head. "Too many mouths already. Be grateful for the boy."

But gratitude was not the feeling she held. Billy had been a colicky, angry child, wailing at nothing and sleeping only when soothed by candlelight and the heavy rhythm of Alice's pacing. The workers said nothing aloud, but more than one crossed themselves when passing his cradle. One morning, a dead bird had been left outside the nursery window, with its wings broken and eyes pecked out.

Alice had found her solace in embroidery, in quiet, in books, and eventually, in Lucy. Lucy, who looked at her with wide, listening eyes. Lucy, who needed no coaxing to learn, who never raised her voice, who reminded Alice of something almost divine: hope returned in a smaller shape.

But Will noticed.

"You're spending an awful lot of time with that girl," he said one evening as they dressed for dinner.

Alice didn't look at him. "She's clever.

And she is sweet. And she needs someone."

"You have a son too."

"I have a boy who stares holes through people and delights in making the chickens scatter."

"He's jealous, Alice."

"He's cruel."

"He's your own flesh."

Alice's face tightened. "And Lucy is my choice."

From that day forward, the tension between them grew palpable. Billy also noticed the tension. He would linger near Lucy in doorways, knock over her tea, and scatter her embroidery thread. Alice caught him once, smearing dirt into Lucy's pillowcase. When confronted, he only smiled.

"Why do you care? She's just one of them," he hissed, jerking his head toward the window, where the cotton fields shimmered in the sun. "You look at her like you should look at me. But you don't." He screamed in a near-hysteria level, "Instead, you look at me like you should look at her, with disdain, Mother."

His face was red with anger she'd never seen from him before.

"Because she is sweet and bright, unlike the other children around here," Alice said coldly. She turned on her heel to leave before she had to witness his wrath, signaling that the argument was finished.

As Alice left the room, she left Billy standing with his arms at his sides, hands balled into fists, his chest rapidly rising and falling, nostrils flaring, and the creaking of his teeth from his clenched jaw.

Relieved at not having a physical confrontation with her son, Alice made her way down the stairs. A third of the way down, Billy stormed by her, his shoulder shoved into her side, nearly knocking her down the remaining flight. Alice clutched the banister with both hands to right herself. Billy continued with his fists clenched, not even once looking back at her. Alice, more frightened by what could have happened than by what did, felt her legs give way to sit on the step behind her. One hand covered her mouth, and the other clutched her pounding heart.

Later that night, the foreman found a dog at the edge of the stream, its tongue severed, its limbs broken and bent like a puppet dropped mid-performance. The eyes had gone white, staring toward the house. Had the dog been watching? It was strange how this happened on the same day that Billy stormed out, angry. "But he would never do something like that to an innocent creature, would he?" she thought. A sudden realization gripped her; she didn't even know her own child anymore.

Warnings appeared around the plantation. Little bundles of red-threaded hair, jars of ash sealed with wax, as if the house itself had begun to ward off something it feared. The workers would not say his name, but they muttered prayers near the steps. Whispers followed Billy through the quarters and the cane fields. They referred to him as "spirit-touched" in hushed tones and crossed themselves when he passed.

Lucy caught sight of it one morning

before the sun had fully risen. She had gone to fetch water from the well when she saw Inez, one of the elder women from the quarters, stooped and sturdy, with deep smile lines etched into her dark skin and eyes that missed nothing. Her gray headwrap was tied in the old way, and her hands moved with the rhythm of someone who had lived long and seen more than most. The faint scent of clove and ash clung to her, remnants of the roots she burned and the prayers she spoke before dawn. A leather pouch of dried herbs hung from her waist, worn soft from years of use, and Lucy knew better than to speak too loudly around her. Inez listened for things others tried to forget, kneeling beside the back steps with a small glass jar in her hands. Inez moved quickly, her eyes scanning the shadows, lips moving in a low chant Lucy couldn't quite hear.

Inside the jar were strands of red thread and something dark, maybe hair or ash. Inez pressed it into the crook where the stone met the wooden step, then poured a line of salt in a crescent around it.

When she looked up and saw Lucy watching, she didn't flinch. She only held a finger to her lips. Then she whispered, "For protection. Not just ours. Yours too."

She stood slowly, smoothed her apron, and walked away, leaving the token her mother had stitched by hand, a cloth that carried warning and warmth behind like a quiet warning no one dared to name.

Lucy mentioned it to Alice. "Ma'am, this isn't something that people do unless they're scared. What are they scared of, Miss Alice?"

Alice had brushed it off at the time. But now, each memory and whisper returned to her conscience like a slow drip. When she gave birth to him, cold air enveloped the birthing room like a shroud. No birds sang that day. The midwife said, "A demon passed over the chimney. Said she saw its shadow stretch across the crib."

The midwife hadn't stayed long afterward. She had left a bundle of sweetgrass and iron nails by the door and refused to come again.

She remembered Will laughing it off

when she tried to remind him during a time years later, when Billy was acting out. "Old superstitions," he had said. "He's just a boy."

But the boy who had once screamed instead of cried now smiled in silence when pain unfolded around him.

Alice forced a smile as she looked down at Lucy. "They just want to make sure everyone is safe. Isn't that sweet?" she said lightly.

But inside, her gut seized. This wasn't sweet. This was pure fear. Thick and pervasive like smoke. In her lifetime, no one had ever uttered prayers or buried protective charms around a child the way they did around Billy.

And it wasn't just superstition anymore.

He had left dead mice in shoes. He had buried another child's doll, its face gouged as if clawed.

One worker caught him crouched beside a hollow log in the orchard, murmuring to it and waiting for a response. Another swore she saw a reflection in the water trough beside him, not Billy's, but something with glowing eyes and a mouth too wide.

No one, not even the bravest among them, stayed long in the attic anymore. Not since the night a worker heard humming from within, the same tune Lucy sometimes sang in her sleep. Not since Billy was found crouched near the rafters, staring at the wall, whispering a name no one recognized.

Some swore they heard the rafters creak at night, as if straining under the weight of something that should not be there, something moving overhead when everyone was in bed.

Inez said, "A baby born on a silent wind, no cry in his mouth, that's the land taking what it's owed. The firstborn don't belong to the mother, not on cursed ground. It marks them early, wraps 'em up in sorrow, and follows 'em all their life. That child ain't just haunted, he's held."

And years later, Alice began to believe it.

CHAPTER 2

Alice found Will on the porch one balmy evening, staring into the dusk. The air was thick with the scent of honeysuckle, but the birds had gone quiet again, just like they always did at this hour. The trees along the edge of the orchard seemed to lean closer after sunset, their shadows longer than they should have been. No one mentioned it. They never did.

"You still won't believe me, will you?" Alice asked

Will turned back to speak to Alice. "About the boy?" That's normal," he said, nodding his head toward the location where the body of the dog was found. He was trying to downplay the incident

"This isn't normal, Will," she implored.

He shook his head and sighed. "You know nothing of the way of boys."

"I do know the way of children; look at Lucy, she's a normal child given her terrible circumstances." She tried not to shout.

"Terrible, terrible?" he stated voice rising, spittle flying from his mouth. "She has become your child, she is getting attention from you, while your own flesh and blood deserves but is refused."

Not wanting to argue where curious ears could hear, she clenched her mouth into a flat smile in silent acknowledgment and walked inside.

Later that night, after Lucy was asleep, Will followed Alice into the parlor, calmer. She sat with her embroidery untouched in her lap, staring into the fire.

"You embarrassed me," he said. "You know how looking amiable in front of them only weakens my authority."

"I protect the one who deserves it," she answered without looking up.

"She's not your blood."

"She is now. In all the ways that matter."

He scoffed. "You're letting sentiment cloud your judgment."

Alice turned slowly to face him, her eyes like steel. "And you're letting pride blind yours. Billy isn't just angry, Will. Something is wrong with him." She shook her head in resignation. "You've seen it too, but you just won't admit it."

"He's our son." That was his way of explanation.

"Yes," she said. "And maybe that's the curse."

Will flinched, his face paled, pupils dilated. It was the first time he had shown fear, not of Alice, but of the truth she had named aloud.

She didn't leave. Instead, she stood up calmly, turned to the window, and pulled the curtains shut with slow, deliberate hands, as if sealing something out or in. The wind outside hissed like the cane fields whispering secrets they were tired of holding. Behind her, Will said nothing.

Later that evening, while Alice stitched by candlelight and the air turned heavy again, Lucy stood quietly by the parlor window, her gaze fixed on the orchard. She couldn't say why, but the trees looked different tonight, taller maybe, or leaning in ways they shouldn't. The wind had died, yet the branches swayed as if they remembered something she didn't. A soft rustling, not of leaves, but something underneath, made her step back. Not fear exactly, but knowing. The kind her mother called bone-deep.

She whispered to herself, "They're waiting for someone."

From the shadows of the hallway outside the parlor, Billy was grinning, not like a boy, but like something that had been waiting for the house to split open. He didn't need to understand it to know: something had shifted.

And now, the land wasn't just listening. It was working through him.

It had marked him from the moment he drew breath, silent and still. He didn't just live on cursed ground. He was its mouth, its hands. The curse wore his skin like a borrowed coat.

Months went by. The house remained unnaturally quiet, not a peaceful quiet, but the kind that held its breath between acts of violence. It was quiet like the forest before a predator strikes. There was nothing natural about it. It was just waiting.

At night, whispers threaded through the walls, never loud enough to understand but impossible to ignore. Shadows moved in the corners where no light reached. Alice often turned, certain someone had entered the room, only to find herself standing alone.

Lucy began avoiding the mirrors. Sometimes they showed more than her reflection. Like a hand behind her shoulder, a figure where no one stood. Once, she saw a mouth moving in the glass, though hers remained still. It was as if the shadowy figures were trying to tell her something, but she was too scared to listen.

Then, one heavy afternoon, the quiet broke. The air hung thick with heat, and Alice had gone upstairs for a brief rest. She woke to the crash of breaking china and a high, thin scream that cut through the stillness like a blade.

Her heart thudded. She ran, skirts clutched in her fists, down the stairs and through the hallway.

In the parlor, Lucy cowered against the wall, one arm raised in a feeble attempt to shield her face. Her other arm hung oddly, twisted at the wrist, and her dress was torn near the shoulder. A cracked teacup lay in shards across the rug, and standing over her, breathing hard, was Billy.

"She dropped it," he spat. "She was in your things again."

Alice didn't speak. She stepped between them, shielding Lucy with her body. Her voice came out low and razor-sharp. "Go to your room. Now."

Billy didn't move. He went to raise his hand in a backhanded motion in Lucy's direction.

"Go," Alice said sternly and louder to Billy.

He flinched at her tone. His mouth curled into a sneer, face morphing into a mask of hate; he stood staring into Lucy's eyes a beat longer. Alice hadn't seen the look, but he did turn and obey, stomping from the room like a sulking beast.

Alice knelt beside Lucy. The child was shaking, her breath coming in tiny gasps. A welt was already forming across her cheek, and blood trickled from her elbow. Alice touched her gently.

"Can you stand?"

Lucy nodded, teeth clenched.

That night, after Alice had cleaned and bound Lucy's wounds, she sat alone in the parlor with only the ticking clock for company. In her lap was the linen handkerchief, now stained with a drop of Lucy's blood. She pressed it to her chest.

Later, while Alice rested and the lamps burned low, Lucy slipped outside and found Inez sitting on the back steps, quiet in the half-dark. The air still felt heavy, as if the scream hadn't quite let go. Lucy stepped out to the back steps where Inez sat alone, her hands still and her eyes fixed on the orchard.

She didn't look up when Lucy approached.

"You never met her," Inez said, her voice low, as if the trees might be listening. "Sibella. She came here with William, not the boy, the father, William Sr. Back before you was even born. Didn't speak much. But she saw more than most."

Lucy sat beside her, quiet, respectful.

"She was the one who raised William Jr.," Inez went on. "After Eleanore gave herself to the stream out back, just after he was born. Folks say she died in childbirth, but that ain't the truth. She made the trade with her life so he could live without the curse. Least for a time. Sibella saw it for what it was. The land wanted blood, and Eleanore gave it hers."

Lucy turned her head. "The land made a trade?"

"Did you not hear? It wanted blood," Inez said. "Grief buried deep in that orchard. The kind that don't rest.

Eleanore's death bought that child a little peace. And Sibella? She spent the rest of her days keeping the dark quiet. Marking thresholds. Speaking the old names. Sewing charms in his blankets."

She reached into her apron and pulled a small pouch of herbs, working her fingers over the seam.

"She raised him like he was her own. And it held for a while. But when Billy was born, something changed. The land woke back up. Sibella was gone by then, passed from old age. Maybe peace. Maybe not."

Lucy's fingers curled around the edge of her skirt.

"Billy was the first born to this land since the curse was quieted. That's what stirred it. The land don't forget the debt. It sees blood before it sees names."

Lucy's voice was barely a whisper. "Can it be stopped?"

Inez shook her head. "Not by us. Not all the way. But it can be held back. That's what you're doing now, same as Sibella did. You light the lamps before the sun goes down. You whisper old names when no one is listening. You carry what your mama gave you and walk softly where others won't. That's how you keep it from spreading. Not just with spells, but with remembering. With care."

They sat in silence after that, the kind that settled in their bones. Out in the orchard, the crows had fallen silent. The trees no longer swayed with the wind. It was the ground that seemed to breathe now.

As night descended on them, Lucy lay quietly in her bed, thinking of the conversation she had with Inez, clutching the cloth her mother had given her. She didn't sleep. Not because of pain of what Billy did, but because she now knew what was watching from the orchard.

That night, she heard the song again, the one that sometimes rose from the trees when no one else was listening. The haunting lullaby that never had a name.

This time, she understood why it sang.

CHAPTER 3

Two days later, Will returned home. The wagon rumbled down the path just before dusk, its wheels kicking up dust and a sense of dread.

Alice stood on the porch, arms folded, the front door open behind her, like a question waiting to be answered. She did not greet him with a welcoming kiss.

"He goes to the river house," she said before his boots hit the first step. "Or I leave."

Will paused, caught off guard by her statement. "You'd send your own son away?"

"He's not safe. Not for her. Not for me

or anyone. And you won't stop him. So I will."

He stared at her, his jaw tightening. "You've made your choice, then."

"I have. And if you ever loved me, truly loved me, you'll honor it."

Behind her, the house seemed to breathe differently. Will could feel it. The shadows felt heavier, and the light harder to hold. But he said nothing more in response.

That night, Billy was sent to stay with Will's brother's family upriver. They had boys near his age, rough and unruly, wild in a way that made Billy look tame by comparison. Will said he'd fit in just fine. Alice said nothing, but inside, she wondered if sending darkness into darkness only sharpened its edges.

He didn't cry. He didn't ask why. He only glared at Lucy as he left, his steel-blue eyes promising something she would never forget.

After the wagon rolled out of sight, the house seemed to breathe again. The air, long pressed tight and watching, loosened. Floorboards stopped creaking without cause. Even the dogs, who had taken to pacing, curled up by the hearth like they used to. It wasn't peace. But it was a letting go. A moment of quiet that felt earned.

Not surprisingly, trouble followed Billy to the river house. Within weeks, whispers drifted back to Cheney Land first of missing tools, of a neighbor's injured dog, and of a shed burned down behind the gristmill. Will's brother sent letters, terse and weary: "He doesn't listen. He runs off at night. The other boys are afraid of him."

The story went that one night, Billy led a group of boys into the woods, claiming he knew where a ghost lived. Only two of the boys returned before dawn, scraped, trembling, and silent. The third boy was found near the creek, confused and bruised, unable or unwilling to say what had happened. After that, Billy was no longer invited to stay indoors. They made him sleep in the barn.

Will never gave Alice the letters to read; he only relayed the barest facts. But even in what he didn't say, Alice heard enough. Darkness didn't disappear just because it changed location. Sometimes, it grew stronger in the shadow.

One night, he sat beside Lucy's bed, stroking her back as the girl drifted into uneasy dreams, her fingers tracing the curve of a lullaby once stitched into memory.

As she sat there, Alice felt the weight of it all. The blood on the handkerchief, the bruises on Lucy's arms, the secrets the house held. Guilt seeped into her chest like a slow poison. She had not chosen this life, not fully. She had been born into it, inherited it like the china and the silver. But still, she had allowed it. Benefited from it. And now, it rotted everything.

She couldn't fix the world. But she could choose what she did with the child before her. Alice had once prayed for a daughter. Perhaps God had answered in the way she least expected.

She would raise Lucy differently. Let her learn. Let her speak. Let her choose. She would give her something more than survival.

CHAPTER 4

Abby was born on a gray morning in late autumn, when the wind carried the scent of chimney smoke, and the cane fields whispered of endings.

Inez was the one at Alice's side, stooped but steady, her hands worn but sure. She'd come from the quarters just before dawn, muttering prayers under her breath as she boiled water and laid out cloth.

Lucy waited just outside the room, clutching the embroidered handkerchief Alice had given her, its threads now softened with time. When the baby's first cry split the air, Lucy didn't flinch; she smiled.

Alice held her daughter to her chest with shaking arms. She had feared she might not live to see her, but there she was, Abigail, named after Alice's mother, with a full head of dark hair and a cry like thunder cracking across the fields.

Will. stood in the corner, silent. He had not spoken a word since the labor began, nor offered comfort. When Abby cried, his eyes narrowed, not in worry, but in calculation. He did not step forward. He only watched.

"She looks like you," Alice whispered, trying to offer something gentle.

Will's lips barely moved. "Now you got what you wanted," he said flatly. His tone carried no joy. Only a bitter echo of something he'd long held in.

Alice said nothing; there was nothing to say to a man who saw a daughter as a debt paid. He turned and left the room without touching the child, laying only a hand on Alice's shoulder as acknowledgment.

That night, as Inez cleaned the linens,

Alice stared at the ceiling and remembered another woman, one she had met only once, just before her wedding to Will.

Sibella.

She'd stood in the kitchen doorway, quiet and watchful. She had not smiled when Alice spoke of children. She'd only said, "Don't let the land take what it's owed." And then she'd vanished, dead within the month. No one ever told Alice how.

But the warning had stuck. And now, with Abby's weight in her arms, Alice wondered what the land would ask next.

Lucy welcomed Mr. William's absence so she could come in to celebrate Abby's arrival.

Lucy held Abby for the first time just hours after she was born. As Alice rested, Lucy sat by the hearth, humming softly.

"You're smaller than a sparrow," she whispered to the bundle in her arms. Abby blinked up, one hand curling around the air.

"But you're strong, I can feel it. You're gonna be just fine, long as I'm near."

She leaned closer, forehead against

Abby's. "I'll be your shadow, baby girl. You cry, I come. You laugh, I laugh. When you get scared, just hold my hand."

From the start, Lucy hovered like a sentinel: watchful, quiet, and ready. She helped warm the cloths, fetched water, and sang soft songs she'd half-remembered from her mother. The baby seemed to calm at Lucy's voice, turning her head with each hum.

Alice watched them both and felt the guilt and grace knot in her chest. Abby was her legacy. But Lucy was her redemption.

That winter, Alice embroidered a new cloth, with forget-me-nots stitched beside tiny canes of sugar and a rising sun in gold thread. It was for Abby, but she pressed it first into Lucy's hand.

"Everything I couldn't fix," she said, "you helped hold together."

Outside, frost gathered on the windowpanes, etching patterns like roots or veins, like the veins beneath red clay. In that house where so much had gone unspoken, two girls, one by blood and one by bond, began to grow side by side.

Lucy took to caring for Abby as if she were her own kin. She rocked her when Alice's arms grew tired, made her laugh with funny faces, and sang the old songs her mother, Eliza, used to hum, letting them weave between the walls of the house like a balm. As Abby grew, she reached first for Lucy, her small fingers curling around Lucy's thumb like a promise.

The two were never far apart. Where Abby toddled, Lucy followed. When Lucy read aloud by the window, Abby climbed into her lap. Some of the older workers whispered that the girls were like mirrored stars, one born of night, the other of dawn, bound together under a sky that remembered every secret.

Alice often watched them from the threshold, hands folded, and thought, "This is how healing begins, not with apologies, but with new roots finding their way through old earth." And the house, old and heavy with memory, held its breath.

Lucy noticed Mr. William would not step foot in the nursery. And that, more than anything, told her the house had chosen whom to protect.

But even in that stillness, darkness left its trace. There were unnatural and cruel deaths on the plantation. The stable boy was found hanging upside down from the rafters, reins wound so tightly around his legs they cut through flesh. Strange, looping marks were scorched into his chest, as if burned by rope or something hotter. Bruises ringed his neck, purple and deep, in the shape of hands too large for any boy his age. His mouth was stuffed with feed, eyes wide open, flies already thick.

The maid who wandered into the orchard was found face down in the creek with scratches torn into her cheeks. Her shoes were missing. Her tongue had been severed. Her nails cracked and broken, one hand still clenching a tuft of light-colored straight hair, as if it had been torn from someone's scalp. The maid was dark-haired. The lock she held was not hers. Some said it looked like Billy's, though he was far away by then. Others said it was Abby's, though that would be impossible.

But in the Cheney House, time did not always move in one direction.

Some said it was a coincidence. Others whispered of curses. Will dismissed the whispers. He called it hysteria, the tales of bruised necks and vanished shoes, the cries in the night. "The help spooks too easily," he said to Alice, though even he had taken to locking the doors more tightly. But late at night, she caught him standing by the parlor window, staring out at the tree line with a tight jaw and a hand clenched around the poker. He refused to speak of it, but he no longer let Abby play near the creek.

Will called for a doctor or a preacher, not a root worker. He buried the maid quietly and warned the staff not to gossip. He said nothing when Lucy began waking in the night, crying, and refused to explain the claw marks on the stair banister that no one had noticed the day before.

But Lucy felt the shift more keenly than anyone. She lay awake at night, listening to the sounds that slipped between the floorboards: moans that didn't follow the wind, footsteps that paused just outside her door. She dreamed of water, rising and dark, and always something beneath it reaching up.

She asked Inez if spirits could follow a child, and Inez only gave her more salt and told her to whisper back to the land. "It knows who you are," she said. "It's listening to you now."

Lucy began marking her windowsills with chalk, as her mother had done before. She braided rosemary and black thread into the hem of her dress. When Abby cried at night, Lucy held her tight and hummed through her own fear. And when Alice came to check on them, Lucy only smiled, even though her fingers trembled.

The house didn't feel like a home anymore. It felt like a mouth, waiting to speak something terrible aloud. But those who had lived on the land long enough remembered Inez's words at Billy's birth: "When the first child comes into the world, the land marks it. And it doesn't forget."

They stopped whistling after dark. A murder of ravens began to roost on the edge of the orchard, watching with eyes too sharp and too knowing. Their cries cut through the silence just before dusk, unsettling even the dogs. And each night, strange noises rose from the fields, moans that seemed too long to be human, cries that sounded like the maid's ragged choking, distant.

The enslaved refused to step outside after sundown, even for firewood. They laid salt at thresholds and whispered charms at their doors. Some claimed they had seen a figure with glowing eyes at the tree line, standing still and watching. They began placing sprigs of rosemary under pillows again. And maybe, just maybe, it would be enough. "You're safe now," she whispered. "As long as I breathe, you're safe," Alice told her girls.

The house had been quiet, yes, but it was a quietness with teeth. Not peaceful, just watching. Holding what it knew like breath in a dark room.

Lucy moved through it like a shadow with purpose, laying small things in hidden places. She whispered when no one listened, and the land, for now, listened back.

Beneath the parlor floor and cellar brick, her marks remained: a coin, a knot, a line of salt, a piece of her mother's cloth, soft with memory and worn from prayer.

She did not know what would become of it all, only that someday, someone would come looking. And when they did, the land would answer.

Not with vengeance, but with memory.

Because nothing buried on cursed ground stays silent forever.

Lucy ensured the story would remember who carried it first.

CHAPTER 5

*L*ucy hadn't touched the bundle in nearly three years. Not since she found it behind the brick in the cellar wall: the coin, the brittle sprig of herb, the parchment with its fading marks. She'd kept it hidden under the floorboard near her bed, never speaking of it to anyone, not even Miss Alice.

Now, as the candle burned low on the dresser, she unfolded the cloth across her lap. Her hands, no longer the unsure ones of a child, moved with reverence. The words on the page, once strange and shapeless, rose clear and sharp beneath her gaze.

Buried beneath the red tree, she was the first the land claimed. Let grief rest where it fell. If the roots are fed wrong, it wakes. If the wrong blood thrives where sorrow was never honored, it rises.

Lucy read the note again, slower this time. The candlelight danced as if reacting to her breath. The meaning had changed, not the ink, but what she could now feel in the marrow of it.

She wasn't the one to end it. But she could sense how the land watched her. How it listened. It knew she carried the truth now.

Her mother's voice echoed in her mind: "If you are quiet, listen to the land. It tells the truth when people won't."

The land had mourned a long time. And now it was angry.

She reached into the bundle and touched the coin. The crescent moon and thorn carved into it matched the mark she had seen at the base of the twisted tree in the orchard—the one everyone avoided.

This was why the ravens had come. Why her dreams had turned. Why Billy had never cried. Because something old and grieving had been stirred. And it had chosen him.

She folded the cloth again and placed it beneath the floorboard. She knew what had to be done. Protect Miss Alice. Protect baby Abby. And keep Billy's evil from leaking past the house.

She would whisper to the land in her mother's cadence, braid thread into the hearth brush, leave petals beneath Abby's cradle, and draw symbols in the flour bin only she could read. Hum the songs her mother taught her and speak the old names only when no one was listening.

She could not undo what had been buried. But she could keep it bound.

In the weeks that followed, Lucy became more deliberate. Going back over all the charms and salt she had laid before, including tying rosemary into knots and leaving them in corners where the air felt colder than it should. She etched circles with spoon handles into soft earth behind the house and murmured the old names into the folds of laundry hanging in the sun.

She never told Alice. Not because she did not trust her, but because she knew Alice already carried too much. Instead, she kept Abby close, cradled her when she fussed, and lulled her to sleep with soft songs that had once come from Eliza's lips.

Lucy vowed that the land would not take Abby. It would not take Alice. Not as long as Lucy breathed.

One morning near the end of summer, Lucy found Inez gathering herbs behind the quarters. The older woman moved slowly, her fingers deftly selecting stems and leaves.

Lucy approached quietly until Inez turned and looked her directly in the eyes.

"You opened it, didn't you?" Inez said without further explanation.

Lucy nodded in acknowledgment. Some things were understood between women without words.

"That bundle comes from Sibella, I reckon. She kept the land quiet for years. Did it with breath and blood, girl. Burned things when the wind shifted wrong. Stitched sigils in her hem. And when the boy was born, she knew it was too late."

Lucy looked down. "I'm trying."

"I know you are. And the land sees that. It's hungry, but it ain't mindless. It knows when a child is trying."

"Can it be undone?" Lucy asked.

"Not by you, child. Not by me, neither. What was done was a mother's grief and the tearing of her people's world. That pain rooted-in deep. Only her own can set her down right. But you? You can keep her from rising too angry. That's what Sibella did. That's what you're doing now."

Inez pressed a small pouch into Lucy's hand. Inside were dried herbs, a small bone charm, and a slip of cloth tied in knotwork.

"Bury this under the eaves. In the south corner. Say the old name if you know it. If not, say your mother's. The land'll understand."

Lucy blinked hard, the weight of it settling into her chest. "I will."

Inez nodded once. "Then go on and

protect them, girls. They're your tether now."

As the days passed, Lucy began to anticipate Alice's movements before she made them. She would place the teacup on the tray just as Alice looked up from her stitching. She would retrieve the book from the shelf that Alice liked best before the woman even asked. Their silences were no longer awkward but filled with a quiet understanding.

In the mornings, Lucy helped dress the baby, her hands careful around Abby's tiny arms. The child gurgled when Lucy entered the room and reached for her with the same familiarity that she had for Alice. Lucy never said it aloud, but she had come to think of Abby as hers too. Not by blood, but by bond, by all the hours spent rocking, humming, and soothing.

They would sit in the garden when the sun was high, Alice stitching and Lucy sorting herbs in her lap. Abby would nap in a cradle nearby, shaded by an old muslin cloth stretched between two chairs. Sometimes, Alice would tell Lucy stories, not grand ones, but small ones, like how her grandmother used to plant lemon balm near the porch to keep away bad spirits, or how certain birds never sang near the orchard.

In those moments, Lucy let herself believe she belonged. That she was not just surviving but living. The handkerchief Alice had given her stayed tucked in her pocket most days, the embroidery growing faint with use, but still full of meaning.

In the afternoons, Lucy practiced stitching her name on scrap linen. At first, her letters wobbled and tilted, but slowly they straightened, as if they too were learning to stand tall. Alice never scolded her mistakes, only offered soft encouragement and more thread.

At night, once the baby had been bathed, fed, and settled in her cradle, Alice would read aloud by the firelight. Lucy listened with her hands folded, memorizing every syllable, storing them deep inside her like seed in dry ground. She had never known words could be beautiful, that books could hold entire worlds.

She learned which herbs made tea for

sleep and which ones eased a fever. She learned how to trim candle wicks so they would not smoke. She learned that lilac meant memory and rosemary meant protection, and she began tucking small sprigs into Abby's blanket, just in case.

The world outside the house was sharp and unforgiving, but inside these walls, at least for a little while, there was warmth. There was routine. There was something like love. Lucy did not speak of her gratitude, but she showed it in the way she folded linens, the way she combed Abby's hair, and the way she smiled softly when Alice handed her a new book.

She still listened to the land. It still spoke. But now, it murmured less of danger and more of watching. Waiting. For now, the house felt quiet. Held. And Lucy, for the first time, felt like she was holding something too precious to keep whole.

But not all nights were quiet.

It started with dreams. Lucy would wake in the middle of the night, her breath shallow, the blanket twisted around her legs. The fire would be low, the coals pulsing like a heartbeat, and the shadows in the corners of the room stretched longer than they should have.

In the dreams, she stood alone in the orchard. The red tree was always there, looming against a sky that never showed sun or stars. Something whispered from beneath it, not words, but sounds like weeping pulled through water. And in the dream, she always walked toward it, no matter how her feet tried to turn away.

Some nights, she would wake to Abby crying, the baby's voice thin and piercing, her face flushed though no fever followed. Once, Lucy found her standing in her cradle, staring toward the window, her tiny hand pressed to the glass as if someone called from outside.

The house itself changed in small ways. The air turned still before storms, heavy with a scent like iron and old leaves. Footsteps echoed on the stairs when no one moved. The scent of ash crept in beneath the parlor door, though no fires burned nearby.

Lucy never said anything to Alice. What could she say? That something in the house had turned its head toward them? That the dreams carried the same cold she felt when Billy used to smile?

Instead, she started to mark the thresholds again. A line of chalk, a pinch of salt, a sachet of rosemary tucked into Abby's cradle. She tied black thread around the legs of the rocking chair. She left a thimble filled with lavender beneath Alice's pillow.

The cloth from her mother remained under her mattress, untouched but never far. Some nights, she held it in her hands as she whispered the old song prayers, really carried through the bloodlines of women who knew how to outlast what tried to swallow them.

The presence never showed its face, but it moved. Lucy felt it. In the walls, in the silence after a door clicked shut, in the way the flame on her bedside candle sometimes tilted as though wind passed by, though the window was closed.

She could not name it. But she knew it watched them. And it waited.

She kept Abby close. She checked on Alice twice each night. She let the dreams come and did not flinch. She was no longer afraid of being hurt.

Now she feared being too late.

That night, after the garden had gone quiet and Abby was asleep, Lucy sat by the window with her knees pulled to her chest. The moonlight spilled across the floor, and for a moment, she let herself go back, back to the Carroll place, before the scream, before the silence.

Her mother stood at the hearth, humming softly as she folded linens. A pot of sweetgrass smoldered in the corner, and the room smelled like mint and ash. Lucy remembered crouching near the edge of the rug, pretending to read while watching her mother's every move.

Eliza moved differently on certain nights. Her steps slowed. Her hum changed key. She would draw symbols on the doorframe with her fingertip dipped in water and salt. One shape always came last, a crescent, thorns curling from its edge.

"What's that one mean?" Lucy had asked once.

"It means speak only what must be known. And leave the rest in the roots."

She had said it without fear, only certainty. That was the last charm she ever taught her. And the last night Lucy saw her smile.

In the dream-memory, her mother turned toward her and lifted the cloth from the dresser. The one with the faded roses. She pressed it to Lucy's chest.

"You keep this near. If the land ever turns loud, or the house goes quiet in the wrong way, you speak low and you braid tight. And if it watches you, don't blink. Just keep breathing and do not run."

CHAPTER 6

Earlier that evening, Abby had looked up from her doll with furrowed brows. "Lucy, do the trees talk to you?"

Lucy crouched beside her. "Not with words. But they remember. And sometimes remembering sounds a lot like talking."

"I think they know my name," Abby whispered.

Lucy tucked a braid behind Abby's ear. "That's why we say it loud to each other. So it stays ours."

Lucy exhaled into the night air, her breath fogging the windowpane. The house behind her settled, wood creaking like old bones.

She reached into her pocket and rubbed the edge of the embroidered cloth. Her mother's scent was gone now, but the memory stayed. And the symbol was etched into her. Not just the fabric. Her.

Alice had not forgotten everything. Not the way Inez stood frozen in the doorway when the first cries should have come and didn't. Not the way she clutched the edge of the cradle like it burned her. Inez had been with the household for many years, quiet and steady, with eyes that seemed to know things before they happened. Alice had taken to her more quickly than she expected. There was a strength in her. A knowing. The day Billy was born, it was Inez who held the cloth to Alice's forehead. The midwife had already fled—too shaken by the cold that filled the room and the silence that followed the birth. But Inez stayed. She whispered to the child even when he did not scream. When the others stepped back, crossing themselves and murmuring, Inez stepped forward.

That night, Alice woke in the dark to find her sitting in the rocker by the cradle, lips moving in words Alice couldn't hear. "Trying to keep it from spreading," she said when Alice asked, eyes never leaving the child.

After that, Alice noticed the rosemary tucked into corners, the chalk marks on the windowsills, the bundles beneath the floorboards. She hadn't questioned them. Not then.

But the warnings hadn't started with Billy's birth.

They started with Sibella.

Alice had only been to the Cheney House once before the wedding. Will had brought her down from Savannah to see the land—proud of the orchard, the porch, the red clay that clung to everything.

But it wasn't the house Alice remembered. It was the woman standing at the edge of the orchard, tall and silent.

Sibella.

Her eyes fixed not on Alice, but something beyond her.

Will introduced her offhandedly. "She helps in the house. Came down with me from town." Then he moved on. Sibella didn't.

That night, as Alice stood alone by the veranda, Sibella approached her. She didn't smile. Her voice was quiet, even.

"Don't have children here," she said. "Not on this land. Not if you can help it."

Alice blinked, startled.

"It takes the first thing it's offered," Sibella added, eyes on the tree line. "And if you're not careful, it will take more than that."

Before Alice could respond, Sibella turned and walked away. She never spoke to her again.

Months later, just after the wedding, word came that Sibella had died of a sudden illness, no details.

Will dismissed it.

But when Alice gave birth to a baby girl who didn't live, and then to a boy who did not cry, when the birds went silent and the fire refused to catch, it wasn't Will's voice she remembered.

It was Sibella's.

Do not have children here.

The next morning, the wind did not blow, but the trees bent anyway. Their branches creaked, low and slow, leaning east as if pushed by something unseen. The pecan tree at the orchard's edge groaned the loudest.

Lucy noticed the crows first. They had begun to roost in strange numbers, lining the fence posts and low branches like sentinels. They did not call out. They watched.

By midday, the hands grew restless. They moved faster through their tasks, glancing toward the orchard with guarded eyes. No one spoke of it directly, but two of the women muttered prayers as they passed the back porch, clutching small bundles in their aprons.

Lucy could feel it too; the air charged like before a storm, though the sky held no clouds. The ground felt soft beneath her shoes, too soft. As if something below had stirred.

She waited until dusk. Then she went alone, cloth in hand, toward the red tree.

Each step felt heavier than the last, the shadows lengthening around her even before the sun had finished falling. The crows shifted as she passed, rustling but never flying away.

When she reached the tree, she knelt at its base and placed the folded cloth on the soil. Inside was a sprig of rosemary, a lock of her own hair, and the token she had kept hidden since she was eight.

She carved the crescent with thorns into the base of the tree using a small bone needle, the same mark her mother had once pressed into salt. The bark gave way easier than it should have.

She whispered the old words not because she fully understood them, but because she remembered the rhythm in her mother's voice.

The air seemed to still. The crows raised their heads in unison. And for a moment, everything held its breath.

Then the branches stopped their groaning. The roots quieted. The orchard went still.

Lucy stood, brushing her skirt free of clay. She turned back toward the house, knowing this would not be the last time she came here.

But tonight, at least, it would rest.

Life had grown easier in the months since Billy left. The house no longer felt like it held its breath. The hands moved more freely, speaking in low tones again, singing while they worked.

Alice laughed more often. Abby smiled in her sleep. Even the dogs, once jumpy and silent, had begun to lounge in the sunlight like they used to.

Lucy noticed the difference most in the way people looked at her. Not with pity or suspicion, but with something like quiet approval. As if they understood, she had held the line while the house waited to exhale.

But peace did not mean safety. Not entirely. There were still nights when the air shifted, when salt had to be laid, and prayers whispered under breath.

That week, a letter arrived from

Albany, addressed in Alice's sister's careful hand. Lucy watched as Alice read it twice at the table, a slow smile spreading across her face.

"My niece is coming to stay," Alice said softly, more to herself than anyone. "Natalie. She's about your age," she added to Lucy. "From up North. Wants to see the country and help with the little one."

She smoothed the letter across her lap and looked out the window toward the orchard, her eyes bright with something close to joy. "It'll be good," she said. "To have another girl in the house. Especially now."

She did not say Billy's name. She didn't have to.

In the weeks that followed, Inez took more time with Lucy, pulling her aside when the others were busy. She taught her how to bind thread around nails soaked in vinegar, how to draw sigils in flour where light did not touch, how to seal a doorway without hammer or lock.

These were not spells from books.

They were older than that. Songs sung under the breath. Names scratched into wood that no one else noticed.

Lucy listened carefully, her hands steady even when her heart raced. Each charm was a small act of war. Each knot a promise.

"This is how we stayed safe," Inez whispered one night. "You think the curse don't know we're here? It does. It watches. But these? These are how we keep it just a little bit hungrier."

Lucy braided these lessons into her daily chores, threads sewn into the hem of her apron, chalk tucked in her pocket, whispers carried on her breath as she lit the lamps. When Billy came back, it would not be enough. But it would be something.

The storm rolled in fast, faster than any Lucy could remember. One moment, the evening air hung thick and still, and the next, wind screamed through the cane fields, snapping branches and bending trees like wet reeds.

Alice was tending to the kitchen fire when the first thunder cracked. Lucy had just finished tucking Abby in for the night. The young child then whimpered, her hands curling into fists.

The rain came hard, slapping against the shutters. Then the candles flickered. Then they died.

Lucy moved without thinking. She scooped Abby from the bed and wrapped her in a quilt, holding her close as the wind howled around the eaves. The room seemed to darken beyond the absence of flame, thick with something pressing in.

The air was heavy. Not just from the storm. From something else.

She crouched in the corner with Abby clutched to her chest and whispered the old songs, protection charms her mother used to hum when soldiers marched down the road or drunk men staggered through the smokehouse door.

Abby calmed slowly, her cries softening to hiccups. Lucy could feel Abby's heartbeat against her own.

When Alice came up with a lamp lit low and wild in her eyes, she found them still curled in the corner, Lucy whispering into Abby's ear, the window marked with salt, and a piece of iron tucked beneath the sill.

"You knew," Alice said, voice trembling.

Lucy only nodded. She had not known what was coming, only that something was. And that Abby could not face it alone.

One night as the moon rose high and the house finally quieted, Lucy found Inez by the hearth, twisting thread between her fingers.

"Tell me about Sibella," Lucy said softly. "What did she know?"

Inez looked at her long and slow, like she was deciding how much to give. Then she nodded once and leaned back in her chair.

"Sibella didn't talk much. But she listened to the land like it was her own heartbeat. She knew where to stand when the roots stirred. Knew what not to plant near the orchard. And she knew the child coming wasn't meant to breathe air."

Lucy swallowed hard. "You mean Mr. William?"

Inez nodded. "The land wants the firstborn. And it tried to speak on that. But no one listened except her. So, she started the binding early. Prayers in the rafters. Bone in the fire ash. Threads around door hinges."

"And it worked?" Lucy asked.

"For a time. But binding ain't banishment. She held the weight so no one else had to. And it broke her."

CHAPTER 7

That night, Abby couldn't sleep. The storm had passed, but the air felt thicker, like the sky hadn't exhaled yet. Lucy, now sixteen, sat on the edge of the bed, rubbing her eyes, whispering the old songs her mother used to hum.

Abby stirred again under the quilt, her eyes wide and searching the dark.

"Lucy?" Abby whispered, her voice small.

"Shh, baby girl, I'm here. Close those eyes."

"But I heard them," Abby said. "They were singing. Outside. In the orchard."

Lucy froze. "You must've been dreaming."

"No. They called my name. I think they want me to come see. The trees do. They glow sometimes, Lucy. They glow like eyes."

Lucy's heart pounded. She rose and walked to the window. The orchard loomed in the dark, fireflies blinking along the fence line. But something felt wrong. The fireflies had gathered unnaturally, clustered near the red tree like they were trying to light a path.

"You stay right here," Lucy said.

"Don't go without me!" Abby begged, eyes wide with fear.

Lucy sighed. She couldn't leave her. "Fine. You stay close, and don't speak unless I tell you."

The orchard whispered louder that night, not just with wind but with weeping—low, guttural, ancestral. Inez had once spoken in hushed tones about the red tree, saying it stood where mothers from the Trail of Tears laid down their daughters when their legs gave out and their cries grew too soft to hear. The land had never been quiet since. It held their sorrow like root rot, like bone memory. And on nights like this, when the sky split with lightning and the wind curled like a scream, their grief rose again—not as rage, but as warning. Lucy felt it in her ribs, the ache of borrowed mourning. Abby, too, must have felt it—that pull, that sadness in the soil dressed up as song.

Together, barefoot and wrapped in shawls, they crept outside. The orchard whispered, its branches swaying though the wind had died, a movement Lucy had seen before. Just like the night Billy was born, they said, when the trees bent for no reason and the crows gathered like sentinels. It was the same warning, only louder now. A strange hum floated on the breeze, not music, exactly, but rhythm. A low, aching melody that curled into Lucy's chest like smoke.

Abby pointed. "There! The eyes!" she said in a whisper.

Lucy followed her gaze. Two faint lights blinked in the trees, hovering just above the ground. Then gone. The hair on the back of her neck stood.

"We shouldn't be here," Lucy murmured. She felt the land turning beneath her feet. Felt it remembering.

Abby clung to her. "They want someone. Don't they?"

Lucy pulled her close. "They're not getting you."

As if in answer, the hum grew louder. The fireflies spun in a circle, then burst apart like sparks. The trees groaned.

Abby whimpered. "Make them stop, Lucy."

Lucy knelt, one hand pressed to the soil. "You listen here," she whispered to the earth. "I know you're angry. I know you lost more than we can ever repay. But this child is not yours. Not now. Not ever."

The ground shivered. The lights in the sky stopped blinking, the hum went deeper.

Lucy stood, scooped Abby into her arms, and turned back toward the house, her grip tight, as if she were wrapping Abby in the words of the lullaby itself: "Lantern high, lantern bright, keep the sorrow from the night." She had no spell to stop what stirred, but she carried light, and sometimes, that was enough. Behind them, the orchard fell still, but not silent. It was waiting. Watching. Remembering.

Later, Abby curled beside her in bed, trembling.

"Lucy? Why me? Why do they sing to me?"

Lucy brushed her hair back. "Because you're young. And kind. And pure. They think that means you're easy to take."

"Am I?"

"No, baby. Not while I still draw breath."

Abby nodded slowly. "Then promise you won't let me go there alone."

Lucy tightened her grip. "I promise. And if they come again, we light the lanterns, remember?"

Abby blinked. "So they can't find us in the dark."

"That's right," Lucy said. "Because we carry light, and they can't take what's already shining."

Lucy held her close and began to hum, soft at first, then with words that had been passed down like thread in the hem of an old dress. Every night, she sang the same lullaby, her voice steady even when her hands shook.

"Hush now, baby, close your eyes. Moonlight walks where sorrow lies. Roots run deep and stars don't stray, Mama's voice will keep you safe.

Candles lit and salt lines drawn, Spirits hush before the dawn. If the wind begins to moan, Know the land won't take its own.

Sleep, my star, where shadows part. Wrapped in thread and held in heart. Braided prayers and breath I send, You are mine until the end.

Lantern high, lantern bright, keep the sorrow from the night. Where the stillness stirs the dead, Let no shadow cross my bed."

Abby never remembered the words fully, but she always sighed heavier after that last line, like even the dark had no choice but to wait outside the door.

CHAPTER 8

The morning sun rose golden and gentle, casting warmth over the land that didn't quite reach the bones. It was the kind of day that might fool a body into thinking nothing had ever gone wrong. But the land remembered. It always did.

Cotton bloomed thick across the fields, soft and swollen. The final harvest was underway, voices rising and falling as the workers moved in rhythm. A cart's wheel groaned in protest somewhere down the slope. The house behind them creaked like it, too, was listening.

Lucy walked with Abby toward the

washbasin near the back porch. Abby's small hand stayed tucked in hers, quiet and damp. She hadn't said much since the night in the orchard, only watched the trees from behind Lucy's skirts.

"They're still out there," she whispered. "Even in the light."

Lucy didn't answer. The trees stood still—but not peacefully.

The porch door slammed behind them.

Mr. William leaned in the doorway, arms folded. "You wanderin' again? Talkin' to trees?"

Abby shrank.

"She stayed close," Lucy said, voice flat. "She was scared."

Mr. William's eyes narrowed. "Then maybe she should be. Sometimes calling things brings 'em."

He stepped past them. Whiskey clung to him like sweat. Lucy waited until he was gone, then knelt beside Abby.

"You don't have to be afraid of his stories," she said. "You listen to me, not him."

But even as she said it, the silence

around the porch pressed in. The birds had gone quiet. The cats had stopped crossing the yard.

Something had shifted. Something was coming.

Far out past the fields, a train whistled long, low, mournful.

Alice paused mid-stitch. Lucy looked up from the basin. Even Abby stopped humming.

Something was coming. Yes.

But not just Billy.

The letter had said she was on her way.

And this time, the house wouldn't keep its secrets. Not with Natalie arriving.

Later that week, just before dusk, Lucy went to the edge of the orchard to gather apples before the frost took them. The wind had gone still, but the leaves rustled at her feet like something trying to flee.

Beneath the red pecan, she saw it.

A deer. Split from throat to belly, ribs cracked like a cradle. Its tongue nailed to the tree. Two stones were carefully and precisely set where its eyes should have been.

She backed away. The clay beneath her feet pulsed with not just dread, but something even darker. Satisfaction.

By morning, it was gone.

No blood. No stones. Only a mark etched in the bark: a crescent with thorns.

She didn't speak of it. But she never entered the orchard alone again.

When the dogs began to bark at nothing, Lucy lit a candle and whispered her mother's prayer to the floorboards.

That night, she heard it again. The voice. Just beneath the hearth's last ember. Breathing, like laughter pulled through wet teeth.

Once, she'd pressed her ear to the wood.

Never again.

One morning, she dusted the mirror above the mantle. Her reflection blinked too slow. Its smile didn't belong to her.

She knocked the firewood basket over and covered the glass with muslin. It stayed covered.

She found claw marks in Abby's bed the next day. Deep. Curved. The kind that came from something that had never been human.

She burned rue and stayed in the nursery all day. Watching.

Waiting.

Not afraid. Not yet. But bracing.

Because the orchard had fallen quiet again.

And that was never a good sign.

BEFORE THE TRACKS
WERE LAID

EPILOGUE

Peachtree Plantation, Georgia, 1863

They said the screams didn't carry past the orchard. The red clay swallowed sound the way it swallowed bodies.

Natalie knew better. Because she heard Lucy's cries before she ever saw the bruises.

The first time they met, Lucy didn't say a word. She was kneeling in the dirt near the root cellar behind the outdoor kitchen, rubbing something into the wood, mud mixed with crushed herbs.

Natalie stood a few feet away, arms

crossed, unsure how to begin. "Does that do anything?" she asked

Lucy didn't look up. "Sometimes."

"You don't talk much, do you?"

"I talk when I have something worth saying."

That shut Natalie up for a moment. She had expected something softer, someone grateful for the help. But Lucy wasn't here to make her feel useful. She was here to survive.

Billy had a way of turning other people's pain into power. A grin that didn't reach his eyes. A temper that twisted rooms into cages.

Even Billy's own parents were afraid of him. William Jr., Natalie's uncle, refused to acknowledge anything was wrong. Alice, his wife, moved through the house like a ghost, always shielding Abby, their daughter, always flinching at sounds that hadn't happened yet.

Billy was tall and well-dressed, with a polished exterior and a predator's gaze. Most folks in the county avoided eye contact. Instinctively.

Natalie didn't. Natalie met his gaze head-on, even when it chilled her.

However, it was Lucy who endured the worst of Billy's abuse. Lucy was quiet, bruised, and enduring. Billy's "favorite," he called her and always with a smirk.

One evening, Natalie found her again, though this time by the creek, rinsing blood from the hem of her dress. Natalie stepped closer to Lucy.

"I could help you," Natalie offered, voice slightly above a whisper

Lucy didn't answer.

"You don't have to stay," Natalie pressed. "There are safe houses. I know people up North. It wouldn't take much. You could vanish."

Lucy wrung the fabric out and looked over her shoulder at Natalie. "I'm not the one who runs."

"Why? Why would you stay and take more of this?" Natalie waved her hands around at the surrounding land.

"Because I still have work to do."

Natalie didn't speak right away. She'd grown up in Albany, in parlors where danger was theoretical, spoken of in newspapers and quiet conversation. But this land—it breathed danger. And Lucy, somehow, stood within it like an unmoving stone in the storm.

They weren't friends. Not yet. But danger can make allies of strangers.

Natalie began to help in small ways. Slipping cloth, shoes, or matches into the pile Alice set aside for "the workers." Asking questions and listening more. Paying attention to the little things happening around her.

One night, while cleaning the kitchen, she asked, "Do you ever feel like you're being watched?"

Lucy didn't flinch. "The orchard watches. Especially at night."

"You believe that?"

"I don't have to believe. I've seen it."

Natalie shivered. "Like what?"

Lucy hesitated, then said, "Eyes. Between the trees. Glowing, just for a moment. Then gone."

Natalie swallowed. "Billy?"

"Worse," Lucy whispered.

Girls were going missing in the county. They were always girls who looked like Lucy. They were always found near the edge of the orchard, or never found at all. One girl had her neck twisted so far around the coroner wouldn't speak of it. They said it couldn't have been an animal. "Animals don't do that."

Not one that walked on four legs.

One evening, Natalie woke to the sound of humming. A lullaby. But no one sang in the house anymore.

She crept to the window. Nothing outside. Just fireflies blinking too slowly. But she felt it, that thick, low pressure behind her neck. The feeling of being watched.

She turned and found Lucy standing in the hallway, holding a candle.

"You heard it too," Lucy said.

Natalie nodded.

After that night, something shifted. They shared a meal together. Sat side by side. Even laughed once when a chicken startled them in the dark.

"I thought you were braver than that," Lucy teased.

"I'm brave when it counts," Natalie said.

"You stayed," Lucy replied. "That counts."

Later, they stood under the awning behind the kitchen, staring into the trees. The firelight didn't reach the orchard, only hinting at its edges.

Natalie's voice was barely above a whisper. "What's worse, Lucy? Billy… or the orchard?" Her gaze slipped over the moss-covered pecan trees, their limbs stretched out like arms searching for something in the night to make their own.

Lucy didn't answer right away. Her eyes stayed fixed on the dark between the pecan trees.

"Billy hurts what he can see," she said finally. "But the orchard? The orchard waits. It remembers. And it always takes something back."

The next day, as they folded linens in the corner of the kitchen, Natalie hesitated, then asked, "Why does Abby cling to you like a sister?"

Lucy smiled faintly. "Because I've been here since she was born. I was the one who sang her to sleep when Alice couldn't."

"But Alice lets her. She lets you hold her like that. Even though…" Natalie trailed off.

"Even though I'm not supposed to," Lucy finished for her and smiled wistfully. "Miss Alice doesn't say it out loud." She straightened herself and continued, "But she knows what this place does to girls. She wants Abby to know safety while she still can."

Natalie's brow furrowed. "And you? Why do you stay so close to her?"

Lucy looked down at her hands. "Because someone once held me like that. Before all this. And because if the orchard ever comes for her, I'll be the first thing it meets."

When Natalie encountered the man with torn boots and a stitched-up cheek, she didn't ask who he was. She wasn't sure, not entirely—but she believed he was running from something. Maybe someone. Lucy said nothing, just nodded once and led him to the root cellar beneath the leaning pecan tree. Natalie followed, silent too, offering a coat and a bit of meat. Whatever this was, it wasn't to be spoken of, and she believed she knew what it was, and she wanted to be a part of it.

Later, as they stood at the kitchen fire, Natalie asked, "Aren't you afraid he'll find out? Billy?"

Lucy poked the embers. "Billy only sees what makes him feel powerful. He doesn't look where he might feel small."

Another night, Natalie found Lucy sitting with her skirt wet, trembling.

"He was watching again," Lucy said.

Natalie sat beside her. "You have to go. You can't keep…"

"He's not the only thing out there," Lucy whispered.

Natalie paused. "What do you mean?"

"Sometimes… the orchard sings. Just before someone disappears. The trees lean in. You can feel it."

Natalie's mouth went dry. "Is that real?"

Lucy nodded. "Real enough."

Natalie wrapped the quilt around her. "Then we keep watch. Together."

They sat in silence, the fire crackling.

Something moved beyond the tree line. Not a deer. Not the wind. A cold breath passed through the clearing, and the trees shivered without moving.

Still, Lucy stayed.

And so did Natalie, not because she had to, but because no one else would.

Because here, in this place of shadows and silence, the girls were stronger together.

Because sometimes the bravest thing a person can do is stay in hell… and hold the door open behind them.

———

Thank you for reading *Before the Tracks Were Laid.*

But the past does not sleep.

Beneath the hush of moss and magnolia, something still stirs.

The land remembers what was done, every secret buried, every cry unheard.

Before the Tracks Were Laid was only the beginning.

In Tracks Beneath the Clay, the roots run deeper, the voices grow louder, and the dead are not finished speaking.

Coming Soon.

ABOUT THE AUTHOR

Leia Kay is a Southern fiction writer whose work draws from the red clay, dark history, and enduring spirit of the Deep South. A mother of four and proud empty nester, she writes stories steeped in legacy, loss, and the quiet power of women who refuse to be forgotten.

When she's not writing, Leia spends her time reading, knitting, and sharing quiet evenings with her husband and her two fluffy fur babies. Her stories walk the line between the living and the haunted, where past and present are always entwined.